MY BEST BREAK

Cynthia's Story

My Best Series
Book 5

CAROLE WOLFE

Blind Vista Press

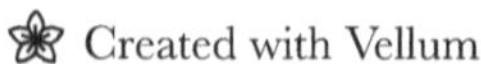 Created with Vellum

Chapter 1

Cynthia Anderson smoothed the black satin dress over her knees. Not too tight or revealing, but the perfect combination of fashion and practicality, it transitioned between awards ceremonies, dates, and funerals. She forgot how fast it wrinkled when she sat though. It was too late now as she was was already at the annual Journalism Awards.

"Just get on with it," she mumbled as she glanced around.

A solitary podium stood on the stage at the front of the hotel meeting room. She wondered if she looked as isolated as that. Even though she'd won last year's award for investigative reporting and had a great chance of repeating her win this year, she hadn't been able to convince anyone to attend the ceremony with her.

Her mother, Cybil, had more important things to do. "My pottery studio isn't going to build itself," she had grumbled when Cynthia asked her to attend the event. "If you had a boyfriend, you could ask him. Or ask your friends. Oh, wait— you don't have any friends, do you?"

A growl slipped out of Cynthia's mouth at the memory, and the woman walking past her shifted away.

Cynthia relaxed her jaw and forced an apology. "Sorry. It's

nerves. I'm up for an award, and I make noises when I'm anxious."

The woman kept her distance but turned back to Cynthia and nodded. "I pick my cuticles when I'm nervous." She revealed a hand covered in a lace glove and fluttered her fingers. "But you'd never know with these."

Cynthia made a face as the woman walked away. Old-fashioned gloves seemed worse than a bad manicure, but each to her own.

With nothing to distract her, Cynthia focused on the empty stage and her solo status.

It didn't bother her that no one from the office had accompanied her. With only five employees, the newspaper was a lean operation. The editor, Dan, had stayed back to cover any stories that might pop up, and Phil, the sports reporter, was at a basketball tournament. The newspaper's customer service rep had tagged along as Phil's photographer.

Truth be told, Cynthia was used to doing things on her own. She knew her intensity could be intimidating to others, but it was the same intensity that made her a good journalist. It let her be honest and open.

Cynthia loved digging up little-known facts. Some people might call it dirt, but someone had to find the truth. She had proven that last year when she won the award for her piece on how local law enforcement agencies ignored repeat DUI offenders.

But that project had nothing on her contest entry this year. Her exposé on an embezzlement case at the Women's Shelter and Support Agency was sure to win. The heart of her story was an exclusive interview with a single mother of three, who had thrived with the help of the organization. The woman's testimony had given the story the emotional draw it needed. Cynthia's efforts had helped end the thefts and kept the agency serving women and children in need.

Cynthia knew she should just be happy she was helping

the community, but there was something in it for her as well: A second win would grab the attention of larger, regional newspapers, generating job opportunities. The *Gazette* was a great steppingstone, but Cynthia wanted something bigger. She needed something bigger. Glen Valley was her hometown, and the *Gazette* had given her the chance to test out her writing skills when she was straight out of college, but she'd outgrown them both in the past twelve years.

A bigger town would have more options. She could find someplace of her own instead of living in her childhood bedroom in her mother's house. No one would know about her past or judge her based on her family. She would be "Cynthia Anderson, reporter," not "Cynthia Anderson, daughter of the town's only single mother."

The announcer's voice cut into Cynthia's thoughts. "Ladies and gentlemen, please take your seats. The twenty-third annual Journalism Awards Ceremony is about to begin."

Cynthia wiggled in her seat. After tonight, she would finally get the respect she deserved. She'd find a job far away from here with an apartment all to herself. She could leave her stuff wherever she wanted and not have to worry about someone else picking it up and trashing it. She would do her own chores when she wanted and how she wanted.

She took a deep breath and focused on the announcer on stage. This was her night.

Chapter 2

Cynthia's face hurt from smiling the entire drive home.

She'd done it—she'd won the award for investigative reporting for the second year in a row.

Cynthia glanced at the trophy on the passenger seat. It would look perfect sitting on her desk in the office. The accompanying bottle of champagne was safely stowed in her trunk, and even though it wasn't her usual drink, she would be happy to deviate from the norm when she got home tonight.

Especially since this win was going to change her life.

Cynthia pulled her rusty sedan close to the curb in front of her childhood home, forced the gearshift into park, and collapsed into the raggedy upholstered seat back. She tilted her head back on the headrest and closed her eyes. If she sat here long enough, maybe her mother would be asleep before she went inside.

Moving back to Glen Valley after college and working at the *Gazette* had been bad enough, but living with her mother, in the same bedroom she'd grown up in, added insult to injury.

"At least it's only for another month," she assured herself.

Her mother's announcement that she was turning

Cynthia's bedroom into a pottery studio still irked her, but with tonight's win, it bothered her less. This award would lead to a new job and a new home. It had to.

Buoyed with her recent victory, Cynthia shook her head as she opened her eyes and grabbed her purse and trophy from the passenger seat. It took two tries to get the car door open, but the trunk lock cooperated, and she retrieved the champagne with minimal fuss.

As she turned toward the house, she noticed her mother's bedroom light was on. Cynthia considered her options: she could sit in the car a little longer, or drive around for a while. But the only place open in Glen Valley at nine o'clock on a Sunday night was the gas station. She didn't need gas, nor did she need a snack. What she really wanted to do was guzzle champagne and bask in her win.

Maybe, if she told her mother about her award, their conversation would be benign. Maybe even pleasant.

Deluding herself wouldn't work in the long run, but it did get her inside the house. Cynthia made it to the kitchen and opened the bottle of champagne before her mother called out, "Is that you, Cynthia?"

"Who else would it be?" she mumbled under her breath as she reached for a wine glass before changing her mind and grabbing a coffee mug. Her mother might think she was having a cup of tea before bed. "Yes. In here."

By the time her mother, Cybil, shuffled into the kitchen carrying her laptop, the champagne bottle was tucked away behind the orange juice in the refrigerator, and Cynthia was seated at the kitchen table, sipping her "tea."

"I need you to post my grades. End of the marking period is tomorrow, and parent-teacher conferences are Thursday and Friday." Cybil looked up and nodded at the mug. "Make me a cup of tea, too. I need something to steady my nerves. Technology is so aggravating."

Cynthia stood up and rolled her eyes. The parents of the

third graders her mother taught were aware of Cybil's technological deficiencies. They dropped in before or after school to talk, not bothering with voicemail messages, texts, or emails. School administration sent requests directly to Cynthia when they needed something that required any form of technology, another drawback of living in a small town where everyone knew each other. Not having to help her mother with her job would be another bonus of moving out.

Cynthia filled the teakettle and put it on the stove, hoping her mother wouldn't notice the kettle was cold. A quick glance told her that Cybil was absorbed with the laptop and not paying much attention. Cynthia got another mug, the tea container, and the honey Cybil preferred.

"Do you have all the grades figured?" Cynthia knew she didn't, that Cybil expected her to input the raw data into the school's online portal, but she asked anyway. This wasn't the first time her mother had waited until the last minute. She took another sip of her champagne to soothe the irritation that was sure to come.

"I wrote the scores in my grade book, just like always," Cybil said. "I don't know why they make me use the silly computer for this. It's faster the old way."

Cynthia knew better than to argue as she measured out the tea into the infuser and placed it in the mug. She listened absently about the dangers of electronics, how students couldn't do math in their heads anymore because of calculators, and how social media should be banned. It was the same spiel she'd heard for years. She wouldn't miss this when she moved out, although she wondered what her mother planned to do for IT assistance when she was gone.

Her mouth opened to ask when the teakettle whistled.

"Shut that thing off. It's giving me a headache," Cybil said.

"Everything gives you a headache," Cynthia mumbled before pouring the water into the mug. She took it and the honey to the kitchen table and placed it next to the laptop. "Where's your stuff? It's late, and I need to get this started."

Her mother nodded her head toward the garage door. "I left it in my car. Go get it for me, will you?"

Cynthia did as she was asked, adding this to the list of things she wouldn't miss when she moved out. She flipped through the grade book to see if it had really been updated, recalling the previous time she'd had to go through stacks of papers to calculate the grades. But she was pleasantly surprised when she discovered it was up-to-date and ready to be inputted.

Her evening was looking up.

Until she walked into the kitchen and saw Cybil taking a sip from the wrong mug. The mug with champagne in it. Before she could say anything, a spray of alcohol shot from her mother's mouth, leaving droplets on the computer and on the table.

"What do you think you're doing, young lady? Alcohol? On a school night? Where did you get this?"

"I'm thirty-five, Mom. It's legal. And *I* don't have school tomorrow; *you* do. I don't have to be at work until eleven, so if I want to have some celebratory wine, I will."

She waited to see if Cybil would make the connection. Her mother knew about the awards ceremony, but Cynthia didn't want to be congratulated out of obligation.

She didn't have to worry.

Cybil unleashed her usual admonition: "What have I told you about drinking? Genetically, it isn't good for you."

Cynthia took the offending mug and gulped down the rest of the champagne. The last thing she wanted tonight was a lecture on her predisposition to various medical conditions and ailments. She understood that it was important to know these things about herself, but it highlighted what was missing in her life: a father.

The high from winning her award had vanished. Ignoring

her mother's continued disdain, Cynthia grabbed the champagne bottle from the fridge and refilled her mug before returning to the kitchen table. She knew better than to argue with the criticism, so, rather than react, Cynthia did what was expected. She took a long sip before she grabbed the grade book and pulled the laptop toward herself.

"Anything else I need to know when I enter these grades? Last time, you neglected to inform me that you'd given the kids participation points for their reading circle."

The long pause made Cynthia look up.

Cybil studied her, a deep furrow of wrinkles resting between her sparse eyebrows.

Cynthia held her breath. Her mother would never be supportive, but she knew better than to antagonize her.

"No. Nothing else," said Cybil, and she pushed herself up from the table, leaving the tea and honey untouched. "I'm going to bed. That Johnson kid is exhausting, and I need all the strength I can get. Put that stuff back in my car when you're finished, and don't forget you need to pick up dinner from Betty's on Thursday. She's doing the schoolteacher special for conferences, and I don't want to miss out on her German potato salad. Eveline always buys it before anyone else can get to it."

Cynthia watched her mother shuffle out of the room without a good night. She didn't expect one.

Nor did she think her mother would ask about the awards ceremony, but it would have been nice to share it with someone.

She topped off her mug of champagne and flipped the grade book open. Might as well enjoy her drink while she got this out of the way. And, noticing the Johnson kid's grades, she knew someone else who might be drinking later this week.

Chapter 3

It was all Cynthia could do not to put her hands over her ears when she walked into the newspaper office the next morning. The normal chaos seemed decibels louder than usual, probably due to a combination of last night's champagne, the conversation with her mother, and a late night of entering grades.

Cynthia hoped the ibuprofen she'd taken before leaving the house would kick in soon. Even if it did, it wouldn't counteract Phil's enthusiasm as he recounted the high-school basketball game from the night before.

"It was flippin' amazing. The kid can do no wrong. He's eight for eight from the free-throw line and made five of six three-point attempts. These kids are phenomenal. There were scouts at the next game against Waverly." Phil nodded over to Cynthia. "You should've come. The recruiters might have been looking for dates."

Cynthia shrugged. "I had better things to do last night—such as winning an award for journalistic excellence."

"You *say* you won an award, but can anyone verify it?" Phil nodded to Jason, the customer service rep who manned the front desk, and smirked. "Sounds like the question, 'If a tree falls in the forest and no one is around to hear it, does it make a sound?' At least if she'd had a date we could confirm the claim."

Jason snorted his agreement.

Cynthia pulled the trophy out of her bag and held it out for them to see. "They don't give these out to just anyone. If you don't believe me, check the Journalism Society's website. The results are listed there."

"I'll look," said Phil.

While he typed, she picked up the foam football that was sitting on a nearby credenza and passed it back and forth between her hands as she said, "They gave a bottle of champagne to the winners as well. It was delicious."

Phil's eyes narrowed. "That explains the hungover look you're sporting . . . which makes more sense than a one-night stand."

Embarrassment and irritation overwhelmed her. She knew she didn't look great, but she didn't like to hear about it. Her grip tightened on the football as she considered her response.

"Be careful," Phil said as his gaze settled on the football in her hands. "You know what happens when you throw things."

The image of the broken coffee carafe popped into her head, the victim of her last poor football toss. She'd had to buy a new one so her boss, Dan, wouldn't find out what she'd done.

Since there was no glass around, she drew her arm back and launched the toy. Phil ducked, and Cynthia cringed when she realized Dan was watching from his office door. The hot-pink-and-purple foam football smacked him in the chest, then dropped like a stone, as if it knew how much trouble it was in.

The office fell silent.

Cynthia chewed on her lip. This was not how she'd expected the morning to unfurl. The last thing she wanted was to upset her editor. Her spirits sank further when Dan turned into his office and called, "Anderson! My office. Now."

It was like being back in high school again. Everyone had teased and taunted her, but when she retaliated, she got in trouble.

"Told ya. You throw like a girl." Phil leaned back in his chair and propped his feet on his desk. "Have fun talkin' to Dan."

"Phil! Get to work!" Dan called out before he slammed the door shut.

Cynthia dashed to her office and dropped off her things before detouring to the kitchen. She pulled one of Dan's favorite energy drinks out of the fridge. She wasn't opposed to using bribes if it kept her out of trouble. Something other than her bad aim must have put her in the firing line. She hoped Dan would take pity on her because her headache was doing a number on her judgment.

"Can I have your office when Dan fires you?" Phil asked as she crossed back through the bullpen. "You have better natural lighting. My African violet needs more sun."

She ignored him as she continued to Dan's office. She knocked and waited. Cynthia knew better than to walk in without permission.

"Enter."

Trust Dan to sound like an aristocrat allowing his servant to enter. Shoving down her growing irritation, Cynthia plastered a neutral expression on her face and walked into the office, determined to handle whatever he might throw at her.

The greeting she got surprised her.

"Hello, dear!" Helene Shaw chirped.

The sound of the columnist's voice intensified Cynthia's headache, and she winced.

"I'm so glad you could join Dan and I."

Under her breath, Cynthia corrected Helene. "'Dan and *me*.' It's an objective pronoun."

"What did you say?" Helene's perfect forehead creased, and she leaned forward.

Cynthia knew full well that Helene had heard her. Helene was just like her mother, asking for clarification to prove some imagined slight.

Okay, this might not be an *imagined* slight, but really? Everyone knew the difference between objective and subjective pronouns, didn't they?

"You sound stuffy," said Helene. "Do you have a cold? Should you really be here at work? You might get the rest of us sick."

"Good morning, Helene. I'm fine." Cynthia ignored the rest of Helene's questions and placed the energy drink on Dan's desk. "What can I do for you this morning?"

Cynthia thought Dan hid a grin when he picked up the drink and popped the top. He took a long sip, nodded for her to sit down, and sat back. Cynthia lowered herself into the chair next to Helene and waited. She'd gotten comfortable with Dan's quirks. The best thing to do was wait until Dan was ready to start.

Helene cleared her throat. Apparently, no one had ever told her it was better to wait than to rush Dan.

A tinge of guilt swept through Cynthia before she caught herself. Helene wasn't her responsibility. Sure, she'd originally brought her in to write the column, but after that, the woman was on her own.

"You know, echinacea is good for a cold. I'll text your mother and see if you have any at home." Helene dug her phone out of her purse and started texting. "Cybil introduced me to a new organic version that worked wonders for Max the last time he was down. Of course, he has to be careful with what types of medications he takes, because we don't want another episode like last year, but the doctor said it was fine."

Cynthia glanced up at Dan. She expected a stern look, but to her surprise, the grin had intensified. The man was actually smiling—at Helene Shaw's ridiculous ramble about a homeopathic drug.

"Mrs. Shaw stopped by with some story ideas this morning," Dan said. "She ran them by me, and I liked them. I've asked her to work with you to get them on the editorial calendar. She doesn't feel comfortable adding her own stories to the productivity app, so I volunteered you as her technical support person."

Cynthia's head whipped up in dismay. That was the last thing she wanted to do right now. Helene was almost as hopeless as Cybil when it came to technology. The last time Helene had added anything to the app, she'd inadvertently deleted the next month's schedule. Cynthia had been able to restore it from backup, but she wasn't interested in reprising her services.

"I'm not an IT person; I'm a staff reporter. Isn't there someone else to help her? Phil? Jason?" Inspiration struck when Cynthia remembered Helene's grandchildren. "Or she could ask Libby or Blake. Kids are good at that sort of thing."

Helene stopped texting and frowned. "Oh. I didn't think of that. That might work."

Cynthia wasn't sure if she was pleased or upset that Helene agreed so quickly, but from the look on Dan's face, Cynthia knew it was a moot point.

"I'm not having grade schoolers use the newspaper's app. Here's your chance to wow me with your skills. And, as you know, the senior reporter position is open. Maybe Phil *is* the better option. Thanks for the drink." He motioned to the door before he turned to his computer and started typing. "Take it to the conference room."

Knowing what she had to do, Cynthia stood up and headed to the door. She waited for Helene, but after listening to Helene thank Dan for the hundredth time for letting her write the wedding column, she rolled her eyes and went to the conference room alone.

At this rate, Cynthia wouldn't need to find an apartment. She could move into a retirement home.

Chapter 4

Cynthia settled into a chair and logged into the conference room computer. While she waited for Helene to finish, Cynthia typed up all the reasons she would make a better senior reporter than Phil. She knew Dan was kidding. He had to be, because she was the two-time award winner, not Phil.

She grinned at the possible job offers last night's win would bring . . . until she remembered Dan hadn't even asked how the awards ceremony went. Her boss didn't seem to care how she'd done.

Her head pounded, but she knew this wasn't the type of pain that could be dulled with ibuprofen.

As she rubbed her temples, Cynthia focused on what she had to do next. Dan wanted her to help Helene, so that's what she would do. It wasn't even that it was difficult; she'd gotten used to Helene's behavior. Helene was a busybody, no question about that; and Cynthia understood how it irritated Helene's daughters, Tasha and Sara. But it was obvious to anyone watching that it was because she loved her family.

Helene had gone out of her way to make Tasha and Greg's wedding a huge success. She had apologized to Sara for interfering in her life and had accepted the fact that her daughter was more comfortable eloping with Jared than having a big celebration. Helene had even gone to therapy with her husband, Max, when they were going through a rough patch.

The term "busybody" also applied to Cybil, but Cynthia didn't think her mother could love anyone. Maybe that was why Cynthia had grown up without a father.

At least, that was Cynthia's best guess about what had happened. Cybil didn't like talking about the past, and as far as she was concerned, the subject was off limits. Not even Cynthia's birth certificate clarified the issue. "Unknown" was written where the father's name should be, which led to some fun conversations when she was younger.

"Was I made like Jesus?" Cynthia had asked after her middle-school lesson on human development. "If you don't know who my dad is, then maybe God put me there."

Her mother had snorted and shook her head. "That's not how it works. There are other ways for babies to be made."

"But the teacher said you needed to be married before babies came. Was she wrong?"

Cybil had shrugged. "Anything can happen in this town."

The sound of Helene's voice jolted Cynthia back to the present.

"Sorry to make you wait," Helene announced as she entered the conference room. "It's so nice to come into the office, but I get carried away when I'm chatting with everyone."

Nodding in agreement, Cynthia waited for Helene to sit down.

When Cynthia had suggested Helene Shaw write a bridal column for the *Gazette*, no one had taken her seriously. Nevertheless, she'd stood by the idea; Helene's knowledge of wedding planning was superb, and she knew everyone in the industry. She connected Darci's Wedding Barn with the

Flower Shop, and, through the grapevine, Cynthia heard each business had since tripled their net profits.

But her coworkers—Phil, in particular—gave Cynthia a hard time for working with Helene.

"Why don't you find some friends your own age?" Phil asked. "You've been in this town forever, so why don't you have more friends? Tasha tolerates you. Sara can't stand you. That receptionist at the law firm pretty much ignores you."

"If you're referring to Renee, she ignores anyone who doesn't understand roller derby, which is the entire town."

Phil considered her comment and then nodded. "You're right on that one. I like watching, though. Heaving your opponent over the rail and not getting in trouble for it is definitely an interesting rule."

Cynthia focused back on Helene when she said, "Thank you again for helping me with this app. I have so many ideas, but I don't know how to schedule them."

Rather than remind Helene how many times she'd explained the process, Cynthia said, "Tell me about the story ideas you have. We might be able to prioritize them as we add them to the system."

Helene nodded. "That would be great. I have so many things I want to cover, but I can't do them all myself." She handed Cynthia a folder. "First of all, Wilbur Duncan bought some property outside of town—you know, the acreage that horrible fast-food place tried to buy. If you let one chain store into the city, the rest are going to take over. Glen Valley *must* stay local. None of those big business ventures coming into town."

Cynthia knew better than to engage in a small-town-versus-big-corporation discussion. The last staff meeting had ended with Phil and Helene arguing about the deterioration of restaurant food. So she flipped through the folder and nodded.

"Looks like he bought a lot of land. What's he planning to do with it?"

"Well, it's not just Wilbur who bought it. Max and I did, and so did Betty. Wilbur and Max went to school together. He happened to be at the bowling alley the other day and shared some nachos with Max." She shook her head. "I know what you're thinking: Max has no business eating nachos at his age, but the doctor says he is as fit as a twenty-year-old these days. A little processed cheese spread on stale tortilla chips with jalapeños won't hurt him every once in a while. At least, that's what Max said the doctor told him. Anyway, Max and Wilbur had a little chat.

"You see, Wilbur's grandson turned ten last month, and there was no place big enough to host his birthday party, so they had it outside in the park, but then it rained. And Max's bowling club had to cram into our living room to celebrate their tournament win. Glen Valley doesn't have enough event space. Used to be that the churches rented out their halls for parties like these, but since my column started, they're booked. Every space in town is booked. So, we're going to build an alternative wedding and party venue."

She didn't think it was entirely because of the column, but Cynthia nodded and let Helene continue.

"Wilbur hired Brad to draw up some plans for additional wedding structures. There's an old farmhouse on one of the properties, which is fine, but some of the girls these days want something fancier. A castle is the first thing on the wish list."

Cynthia laughed. "Brad is designing a castle? Please tell me it doesn't include a moat and alligators. Not sure how that fits with the Glen Valley vibe."

Helene's eyes widened. "That is a brilliant idea! We'd be the only place in the state that offers an exclusive wedding moat." She jotted something in her notebook. "No alligators, though. We'd want swans to swim around and around the castle. Or, better yet, maybe we make it a lazy river so it can double as a water park during the week. Cynthia, you should consider joining us. We could use some investors."

If she had spare cash, Cynthia would be using it to buy her own home, although the wedding venue did seem like a smart move.

"Why don't you ask your daughter?" asked Cynthia. "She's the one who won the lottery."

"Of course, I've told Tasha about our plans, but I'd never ask her for money. I've learned my lesson." She looked back down at her notes. "Max and I are building a bed-and-breakfast. I thought about doing more of a Cape Cod look, but I think something to go with the castle theme might work. Maybe a stable. Each 'stall' could be a room."

Cynthia pulled up the folder to hide the expression on her face. Paying money to stay in a horse stall was the last thing she would do.

"Betty plans to add a café to serve the folks staying at the bed-and-breakfast. Plus, she and Brad are designing a huge catering kitchen in the back so she can handle any wedding buffet or dinner requests. I talked her out of offering wedding cakes, though. The bakery in Travis County said she would rent out a spot in Betty's for exclusivity."

It dawned on Cynthia this wasn't just a whim. Helene had put a lot of thought and time into researching the plan.

Before she could congratulate Helene on the effort, Helene put her hands on the table and gave her a serious look. "I need to apologize for this next part, though."

"What's there to apologize for? This all sounds wonderful. It will bring business to town. Even the newspaper can get involved by printing invitations and programs. I'm sure Dan might have some ideas as well."

Helene beamed. "I hadn't thought of that. This is the reason Dan wanted me to talk to you."

When she twisted the one-and-a-half-carat princess-cut

diamond on her ring finger, Cynthia knew something else was up. Helene only fidgeted when she was nervous.

"There is something else, though, dear. It's the reason I apologized. You see, your mother is going to be part of the project as well."

Chapter 5

For the life of her, Cynthia didn't understand how her mother could contribute to a wedding venue. She couldn't cook to save her life. Hospitality wasn't one of Cybil's strong suits, so hosting at the bed-and-breakfast or helping with weddings wasn't an option. The only thing that Cybil was good at was pottery.

A flicker of nerves arose in Cynthia.

"What will my mother be doing?"

Helene twisted her ring two more times before she answered. "Cybil will be providing one-of-a-kind gifts at the boutique. Pottery gifts. She's also planning to host pottery wheel lessons for guests looking for something unique to do during down time. That's why she's eager for you to clear out of your bedroom." Helene rushed to continue. "Between us, we're planning to make Glen Valley the wedding capital of Quinn County. It will create jobs, increase visibility, and generate income for the town."

Swallowing the lump in her throat, Cynthia nodded. Even though she should be used to being left out, it hurt to find out about her mother's plans from someone else. At least her mother would be so busy that she wouldn't be around much.

And Cynthia had needed to find somewhere else to live anyway.

"Dan said you had some other ideas. Are they in here too?" Cynthia needed a distraction from the hurt of her mother's secrecy. She turned to another page in the folder. "What's this wedding dress database about?"

If Helene sensed that Cynthia was changing the subject, she didn't let on, and they continued through the folder. Cynthia entered each one into the newspaper's productivity app, prioritizing the ones she thought would be most interesting to their readers. When they came to Helene's pitch for a premarital counseling column, it went to the top of the list.

"Dr. Austen, the counselor Max and I see, has already agreed to meet with me and take me through the process. She worked miracles for our marriage, and I want to repay the favor by getting her some publicity for her practice. If she's as good at preparing people for marriage as she is at saving them, the column will be a huge hit." Helene paused when she came to the last item in the folder. "Now, this last idea is for you. You are the perfect reporter to investigate this."

Cynthia's eyes flew to meet Helene's. Finally, someone was going to acknowledge the award she'd won the previous evening.

"And why's that?" she asked, keeping the grin off her face.

"You're the right age for this sort of thing, and you're not ready to start a family."

Helene twisted the ring on her finger again, and Cynthia frowned. Whatever Helene planned to say had nothing to do with winning an award.

"Two important qualities of someone who will be undergoing egg retrieval."

"Excuse me?" Cynthia sputtered. Had she heard Helene correctly? That she was old and alone? Her mother reminded her of this regularly, but having someone else say it hurt a little more.

"Before you say anything, let me explain."

Cynthia nodded because she didn't know what else to do.

"Part of the marriage process can be starting a family. Since people are marrying at an older age, it's harder to get pregnant. Egg retrieval is a way that couples prolong their childbearing years. If you decide marriage isn't in the cards, you can always donate your eggs. Lots of people need this kind of help. Take Carlton and Brad, for example—they've had a horrible time in the surrogacy process."

The reminder about the chiropractor and the architect took some of the sting out of Helene's comments, but Cynthia wasn't convinced. "Makes me feel like an old maid, though."

Helene smiled. "You'll get over it when you win your third investigative reporting award."

Cynthia's mouth fell open, and she blinked back the tears she felt filling her eyes. Her reaction irritated her, but she was happy someone knew about her win.

"How did you find out?"

"Max helped me look up the results this morning before I came into the office," Helene said. She pulled a tissue out of her purse and offered it. Cynthia dabbed at her eyes as Helene continued. "I know this isn't a finance or corruption story, but it *is* a story that affects a lot of people your age. And there are some unscrupulous medical practitioners out there who prey on people desperate for families, so I was hoping this might be something you would be interested in." She pulled another folder out of her bag and slid it to Cynthia. "I've already done some initial research. You'll want to do more, but that should get you started. To be clear, I'm not saying you have to go through with the procedure, but if you did, the article would have a unique first-person spin to it."

Cynthia glanced through the folder, but she wasn't reading the words. The possibility of a third win excited her. She might not need it—last night's award might be enough to get her out of town, but if it didn't, she would have a backup plan. And if there was one thing she'd learned from all her investigative reporting, it was that things went south when all the options hadn't been explored.

She didn't need to think about this. She needed to embrace it.

"I'll do it. The procedure and all. I have no intention of starting a family," she said as she closed the folder, "but this is a great story. I appreciate you thinking of me."

Helene pulled her into a hug. As Cynthia squirmed uncomfortably in Helene's arms, Helene squeezed her.

"Dan was sure you were going to say no. I knew you were up to the challenge."

Glad that Helene couldn't see her face, Cynthia wondered why Dan didn't understand how much success meant to her and how willing she was to work and sacrifice for it. It occurred to her as well that her mother might not approve of the plan. That thought was another reason she should do it.

Pulling away from Helene, Cynthia turned back to the keyboard. "Let's get a couple of deadlines down to keep us on track, and then I think we need to get back to work. We've got a lot on our plates."

Chapter 6

Cynthia didn't realize how true her words were. The next few days were a whirl of researching egg-harvesting facilities, scheduling doctor appointments, and reassuring Dan that she was doing this for the right reasons. For the third day in a row, Cynthia listened to Dan's concerns.

"This is a medical procedure. Complications are common. You might not even have viable eggs to harvest." Dan leaned on his desk, his fingers clasped together. "Plus, the newspaper's health insurance doesn't allow for this sort of thing."

Her conversation with Helene had tipped her off that Dan might balk, so Cynthia had prepared for as many arguments as she could think of.

"That's where you're wrong." Cynthia had checked into the *Gazette's* insurance plan. "I confirmed today that there is a $20,000 provision for infertility treatments, including egg retrieval, and I have a list of doctors who accept our coverage." She held up her notes. "With ten offices to choose from in the tri-county area, this is going to work."

Dan leaned back in his chair. "I don't like it. Seems like an unnecessary risk, if you ask me."

Cynthia tried a different tack. "This is going to be great exposure for the *Gazette*. What other newspaper in the state boasts a two-time winning investigative journalist exploring the alternative and sometimes difficult quest for conception?"

Dan gave a slight nod. "Hmm. Interesting how many times you can work that into normal conversation." He'd congratulated her on the win after her meeting with Helene earlier in the week and admired her trophy. "Phil's asked me several times how he can win an award like that."

"He covers sports. There aren't a lot of investigative reporting awards that sports journalists qualify for."

"There was a guy in Haws County who locked a bowling team in a meat locker so he could win a bet he placed on their opponents. That would qualify, right?"

"Don't give him any suggestions. I'm afraid he might do something rash."

Cynthia's cell phone chimed, signaling an incoming text from her mother. She glanced down at her phone and noticed the time. She didn't have to read the text to know what her mother had written. Dan didn't either.

"Get out of here," said Dan, waving at the door. "Cybil will have your head if you miss the schoolteacher special tonight."

Cynthia chuckled and promised to get back to him with a draft of her column on the egg retrieval process. She got out of the office in record time, mostly because Phil and Jason had left early to cover the bowling tournament.

Hers was the only car in Betty's parking lot, and a quick glance at the clock told her she'd barely made it before closing. Cynthia hurried inside. The last thing she needed was her mother's wrath to be unleashed, especially during parent-teacher conferences week.

She scanned the counter to see what delicacies Betty had to offer. Unfortunately, that late in the day, the pickings were slim. Other than the mustard potato salad, there didn't seem to be anything left that her mother would consider eating.

"I should have left sooner," Cynthia muttered to herself as she concluded a trip to the grocery store was in her immediate future. She turned to go as Betty emerged from the back room.

"Where do you think you're going?" the owner of the coffee bar asked. "Planning to sneak out of here without saying hello?"

Cynthia returned to the counter and sighed. "Sorry." She swept a hand at the counter. "You sold out of things today, which is good for you and bad for me. Mom requested the schoolteacher special, but I see I'm out of luck."

Betty crossed her arms and leaned against the counter. "She told you about this on Monday, didn't she?"

"Sunday, actually. I had it on my calendar," said Cynthia as she threw up her hands. "But I've been busy, and I had a meeting tonight with Dan, and time slipped away." She ran her hands through her hair. "Any suggestions on what I should get at the store to make up for this?"

"Spoken like an adult who is still living with her mother." Betty turned and opened the refrigerator behind her.

Cynthia stared in envy at the neatly stacked boxes of food. Anything in there would be better than whatever she could come up with.

Betty grabbed several boxes and set them on the counter. "Only because I know how intense you get when you're working on a new story was I willing to save a special for you. And Cybil."

Cynthia's eyes got big. "How did you know I've got a new story?"

Betty waved her hand. "Psh. Helene couldn't keep a secret if her life depended on it. Besides, she told me it would be your best break into the major markets." Betty grabbed a paper bag emblazoned with her logo and carefully loaded the boxes into it. "I don't want to be the one who keeps you from winning a third journalism award . . . although I think it might be more important to find a date, especially if you've got harvested eggs to fertilize."

Cynthia blushed at Betty's innuendo. "Actually, I need a place to live more than a date. I've got less than a month left before my bedroom is renovated into a pottery studio."

"I'm sorry to say I'm counting down the days. I can't wait to take a lesson," Betty confessed, adding a few more items to the bag before she turned back to Cynthia. "You know, I heard Mary Beth Andrews is renting out the apartment over her garage. Her previous tenant met his soulmate at the county hoedown, and he left without giving notice. Have you talked to her about the space?"

She had heard about it, but considering her history with Mary Beth's son, she'd ignored the opportunity. Desperation lowered standards, though, so she might have to suck up what little pride she had left and investigate it. Not that she planned to tell Betty.

"Thanks for the tip." She nodded at the bag. "What are we eating tonight?"

Betty's eyebrow raised, and Cynthia tensed, expecting an interrogation about her lack of enthusiasm about a housing possibility. Cynthia had spent the last three months turning over every stone looking for a place to live, and this news should have been exciting. If it were anyone else's house, it would have been. She waited, hoping Betty wouldn't pursue the topic.

Cynthia relaxed when Betty said, "Pork roast with fingerling potatoes, wedge salad, and homemade crème brûlée for dessert."

Her mouth started watering, and Cynthia wondered if she could eat her dessert on the way home. Betty must have known what she was thinking, because no sooner had she slid the boxes into the bag than she stapled it shut.

"Straight home and put the pork and potatoes in the oven at 250 and check it every five or so minutes. Do *not* put the salad in the oven—that will end badly. And do I need to remind you of the Styrofoam container incident from Thanksgiving?"

Cynthia shuddered. The smell had been horrible, and it had taken days for her to clean the oven to her mother's standards, which, of course, was repeated to every person her mother ran into from Thanksgiving to Easter. It was only the fact that Tasha Gerome White put the Easter ham in the oven with the plastic still on that had gotten Cynthia out of the hot seat.

"How could I forget?" She pulled her wallet out of her purse, but Betty shook her head.

"PTO picked up the tab for everyone's dinners. Be sure to tell your mom so she can thank them."

Knowing Cybil would do nothing of the sort, Cynthia made a mental note to work this into the next education article she wrote for the *Gazette*. A little positive publicity for both the PTO and Betty's Coffee Bar would go a long way.

Betty raised her eyebrow. "If I were you, I wouldn't mention this in the newspaper. Eveline Gerome is on a rampage lately, and that might set her off. She and Roger don't think teachers should get any special treatment."

"But you deserve some publicity for this." She didn't blame Betty for not wanting to deal with Eveline and Roger Gerome. It was a well-known fact that Eveline didn't think anyone deserved anything except her and her family. Most people in town tolerated the Geromes because they had to, but Cynthia had never liked them. Mr. Gerome gave her the creeps, and Mrs. Gerome was a pretentious snob. Cynthia laughed a little when she remembered how she'd told the woman off a few months back. It was childish, but it felt good.

Betty's eyes twinkled. "I'll get publicity. Don't worry about that. What I don't want is Eveline marching in here and causing a ruckus." She waved toward the door. "Now, get out of here and feed your mother. She's a monster when she's hungry."

Chapter 7

Cynthia's stomach rumbled as the passenger-side tire bumped the curb in front of her mother's house. Hunger overrode any of Cybil's warnings about improper parking. She fumbled with the bags of food Betty had stapled closed, mentally commending Betty on the decision. If the bags hadn't been closed, she would have eaten her fill on the way home and dealt with her mother's fury.

Not only would her mother have been furious that the schoolteacher special hadn't made it home, but Cybil despised it when Cynthia ate in the car.

"How uncouth can you get? Think of all the food that gets dropped in the car. And you wonder why your vehicle is so shabby."

But she had some time before Cybil got home, so she grabbed her purse and tote and hurried inside. She dumped everything on the kitchen table and turned the oven on to 350 degrees before she remembered Betty's instructions and reduced the temperature. If she burned this dinner, she would never hear the end of it.

She opened the first bag of food and pulled out a sheet of Betty's Coffee Bar stationery. Cynthia grinned. Betty had sent her home with an idiot-proof list of instructions. Rather than feeling bad about needing that much help, she felt relief. It was nice to have someone watching out for her once in a while.

After she followed all the directions, including, *"Set the table with real plates and silverware (none of that plastic crap) and open a bottle of pinot gris. It's a school night, but your mother needs it. She meets with the Thompsons tonight,"* Cynthia poured herself a glass of wine and settled herself in the armchair in the living room. Cybil would have a fit if she found her relaxing with wine before dinner, but Cynthia would be able to hear her mother when she opened the garage door.

She sipped the wine as she considered Betty's suggestion about Mary Beth Andrews's apartment. The location was convenient to the newspaper office, although Glen Valley was so small that pretty much any place in town was close to work. Mrs. Andrews was a sweet woman who never failed to offer a compliment. She'd even emailed Cynthia this week, congratulating her on her win at the journalism award. Cynthia heard from previous tenants that the place was immaculate, and Mrs. Andrews was a fair and gracious landlady.

What kept Cynthia from jumping on the opportunity was the landlady's son, Mark. She snuggled back into the comfort of the armchair as she recalled her first and last crush.

She'd been careful to keep her infatuation a secret. No one knew she'd carried a torch for him.

And probably still did.

Having a mother with trust issues had taught her not to share information with other people that might come back to hurt you. Not that Mark would have ever intentionally hurt her. He was too nice for that.

Having a locker right next to Mark's for four years of high school gave her a front-row seat to see what she was missing. The captain of the basketball and baseball teams entertained a large crowd of friends between classes. Girlfriends came and went, but Cynthia watched how he always treated them with respect, as opposed to other boys his age. He was one of the good guys.

Even though he was above her social status, they'd talked regularly. He hadn't let any of his friends make fun of her. Cynthia remembered the time someone said something mean about the scarf she was wearing; Mark had unwrapped it from her neck and draped it around his own.

"This scarf is awesome—so awesome that I'm wearing it for the rest of the week."

And he had. Even though she'd told him after school he didn't have to.

"My mom's gonna wonder what happened to it. I kinda need it back."

Mark had shaken his head. "Tell me why."

"Why what?"

"Why your mom wants you to wear a butt-ugly scarf like this."

She'd laughed. "I knew you hated it. Why are you defending me?"

He shook his head and pointed at her. "You first. Why are you wearing this"—he struggled for words before he said—"monstrosity?"

If she had any hopes of getting the scarf back, she needed to tell him the truth.

"My mother made it. She's into knitting right now. Last winter, it was macrame. I'd be happy to share the plant hangers she made me if you want. The scarf is an improvement, and more practical since I can't keep plants alive."

Cynthia took a sip of wine but realized the glass was empty. That's what she got for reminiscing. It had to mean that she shouldn't consider calling Mrs. Andrews about the available apartment. She was over Mark now, but that didn't mean she wanted to relive her teenage years and hear about how great Mark was doing or how wonderful his girlfriend was.

She scrunched up her nose at the thought of the last girl-friend he'd brought to town. Usually Mark's taste was impeccable, but this woman had been less desirable than anyone Cynthia had ever met. And that was putting it politely. The woman had made Medusa look friendly.

Cynthia uncurled herself from the couch and made her way back to the kitchen. She poured herself another glass of wine, wondering if Mark was still dating the woman he'd brought to his mother's sixtieth birthday party.

Cynthia remembered her well. Jessie wasn't like anyone Mark had dated in high school. Cynthia guessed that was because they weren't in high school anymore, but it seemed odd that Mark would enjoy spending time with someone who was interested in nothing and nobody but herself.

When Cynthia had volunteered to write the *Gazette's* standard birthday feature profiling Mrs. Andrews, she'd hoped to get some one-on-one time with Mark. They'd met at Betty's Coffee Bar, a neutral location, so she could gather the necessary information. She'd been looking forward to catching up with Mark until she got there and saw a woman by his side—a woman who ended up being his girlfriend. She shuddered when she remembered how rude Jessie had been when she found out that they'd been classmates in high school.

"Marky-sparky, how do you know her again?"

The nickname had made Cynthia flinch. She expected him to joke about the ridiculous endearment, but instead he'd said, "Cynthia and I went to high school together, Jessie. She's a reporter with the local paper, which does birthday features on all its residents. I'm giving her some information, although she knows my mom as well as her own."

Jessie had assessed Cynthia from head to toe, as if determining what risk she posed. When she finally shrugged, Cynthia knew she'd been found lacking. It hadn't taken long for Jessie to get bored with the conversation and wander off to Betty's gift shop.

"Sorry about Jessie. She's not big on small towns," Mark had said as Cynthia slid her notepad and pen into her brief-case, "or moms, apparently. She and my mom had a rough morning. Something about Mom's coffee being too strong."

"I don't see how that's possible. I remember her hot chocolate—she always put marshmallows in it." Cynthia laughed. "Remember how she helped me with my science project junior year when my mom refused? I got all the hot chocolate I could drink for a week. Plus, a better grade than you!"

"That's because my volcano wouldn't erupt. But yours released the perfect amount of lava. Leave it to Mom to be precise." He laughed, then sobered. "Anyway, this is the first time Jessie's met my mom, and she's already asked to cut the weekend short."

The admission made Cynthia sad. The old Mark wouldn't have changed his plans for a woman, but this wasn't high school.

"Unfortunately, Mom overheard the conversation and said if Jessie was so childish and self-centered, she should leave."

Cynthia had kept her face neutral. Mrs. Andrews was the nicest, most patient person she knew. It was completely out of character for her to dislike someone, but Cynthia agreed with Mrs. Andrews. Jessie could have been more supportive and not made things awkward between Mark and his mom.

The garage door opened and startled Cynthia. Cybil was home, and it was time to get dinner ready and tell her about the new story she was working on. Her mother didn't need to know about the possible apartment, or Cybil would call Mrs. Andrews and make the arrangements herself.

Chapter 8

"Good. You remembered to go by Betty's," Cybil said when she walked into the kitchen.

Cynthia watched as her mother hung her purse and school bag on the hook by the garage door and pulled off her sweatshirt.

"There better be wine. That Thompson family—well, let's just say I'm glad this is the last one. You'd think by the fifth kid their parenting skills would have improved, but, no, they're all hellions."

Cynthia considered commenting on her mother's parenting skills but instead grabbed another wine glass and poured her mother a serving. She held it out to her and said, "Dinner's ready when you are."

"Hold your horses. Let me relax first." Cybil drained her glass in one swallow, then grabbed the wine bottle and examined it. "You shouldn't drink alone, you know. Definitely not this much. Have I taught you nothing? Please tell me you're hydrating between glasses."

Rolling her eyes, Cynthia shook her head. "I've only had one glass."

Cybil poured the rest of the wine into her glass, shaking

the bottle to get every drop. "There are four servings per bottle, young lady. I had two and you had two. And you wonder why you live at home. Drink my wine. Eat my food. Take up space."

Instead of taking the bait, Cynthia took the salads she'd already plated out of the refrigerator. "Where would you like to eat your salad?"

Cybil took the plate out of her hand and sidled up to the breakfast counter. She looked around. "Am I supposed to eat with my hands?"

Thinking that shoving the salad down her mother's throat would be a better option, Cynthia retrieved a fork and napkin. She gave them to Cybil and then filled the water glasses with ice and filtered water before being asked.

Once everything was placed on the counter, Cynthia nodded. "Anything else I can get you?"

Cybil shook her head, her mouth already full of lettuce.

Grateful for the quiet, Cynthia picked up her own fork and ate standing up. She knew her mother would complain, but if she sat down, Cybil would ask for something else. It was a lose-lose situation.

After a few bites, Cynthia decided it was safe to return to her question. "Other than the Thompsons, how did things go?"

Cybil took a sip of wine before answering. "Fine. Ida May said my grades weren't in on time, but I told her you submitted them Sunday. She told me to tell you to check my email. They changed the protocol again, and you need to redo them using the new specs." She stabbed at the salad, then nodded at the empty plate in front of Cynthia. "I was planning to have this for lunch tomorrow as well. Guess I'm stuck with peanut butter and jelly again."

Her mother's tendency to martyrdom hit a nerve.

"You hate leftovers."

"I hate *your* leftovers. You're a terrible cook. Makes me

wonder if you're really my daughter sometimes. My rhubarb pie recipe is an award winner."

Knowing she was treading on thin ice, Cynthia opened the oven and pulled out the pork and potatoes. The smell of herbs filled the kitchen, making her stomach growl. She grabbed two plates and made a big production of dishing up the portions before turning back to her mother.

"You got fourth place in the beginner's section, Mom. First place was for a s'more. Not sure that's a great reference for you."

Cybil snatched the plate out of her hands. "I bet you dried out the pork. Betty overcooks hers anyway. And what's this?" she asked, pointing to the potatoes. "I wanted German potato salad."

Cynthia slammed the oven door shut to keep from reminding her mother that this was a free meal cooked by someone else and she should be grateful.

"Watch what you're doing," said Cybil. "I don't have the money to replace appliances."

She tensed at her mother's rebuke and narrowed her eyes. "But you have money to convert my bedroom to a pottery studio. Something doesn't sound right about that. Or did I misunderstand somehow?"

Cybil ignored her and cut into the meat.

Rather than wait for her mother's next complaint, Cynthia cut into her own meal and shoved a piece of food in her mouth. The almond-and-herb-crusted pork melted in her mouth, and the argument with her mother was forgotten while she enjoyed her dinner. Everything tasted wonderful, which surprised her considering it was reheated. What would it taste like fresh from the oven?

"Fresh from the Oven" would make a good title for a column. As soon as she was finished with dinner, she would send Dan an email to find out if she could approach Betty. Even if Betty didn't want to write the column, Cynthia knew the deli owner would be willing to include recipes. Cynthia could interview Betty each week and include the menu plan for dinner. Maybe Betty could sell bags with all the ingredients in them. Readers could buy a bag, then follow the instructions in the newspaper.

It was a great idea if she said so herself. It might be more popular than Helene's wedding column. Everyone had to eat, after all.

"Are you listening to me?" Cybil's voice interrupted her thoughts. "Or are you thinking about another one of your column ideas?"

"What if I am?" Cynthia grabbed her mother's empty plate and put it with her own in the dishwasher. "I do have a job, you know."

Cybil snatched her wine glass off the counter. "Yes, we all know. My students regularly remind me of the fact that my daughter is the reporter who writes the mean articles about people."

Sighing in frustration, Cynthia threw her hands in the air. "I wrote one thing—a year ago—and you keep bringing it up. And it wasn't my fault. Someone gave me bad information." She shook her head at her mistake. No one in town believed anything Doug Gerome did, so she should have been more careful about taking information from him. "It's only Blake and Libby Gerome who remind you, and that's because it was an article about their aunt."

"You should have known better than to believe Doug. He's a liar through and through," Cybil said before mumbling, "just like his father."

"Why do you always say that? Roger Gerome is an icon in this town. If he ever finds out you talk about him behind his back, you've got a problem."

"You're the only one who knows what I say, so I'll definitely know who told him." She rubbed her stomach. "I'm still hungry. What's for dessert?"

"Crème brûlée." Cynthia pulled the treat out of the fridge and read through Betty's instructions for serving it. "It's going to take a few minutes."

Cybil pushed back from the stool. "You can bring it to me in the living room. I'm going to catch up on the news. Maybe there will be a feature on a schoolteacher who makes a difference in the lives of children instead of something stupid like how to pick out the perfect wedding dress or make food that someone else can heat up and call their own."

Cynthia followed her mother. "That's what you're mad at? That Helene has a column in the *Gazette*?"

"Among other things." Cybil lowered herself into the recliner and popped up the footrest. "You just admitted you were thinking about another story idea. I'll bet it has something to do with Betty and her food."

Refusing to give her mother the satisfaction of knowing she'd guessed correctly, Cynthia deflected. "It doesn't matter what I'm planning. What matters is you make a big deal out of everything and then walk away. You don't even attempt to resolve these silly arguments."

"Silly?" Cybil turned to stare at her. "Why is it silly to think my own daughter should be proud I'm starting a new business venture after a thirty-five-year career teaching schoolchildren? There isn't anything silly about that. Why can't you appreciate all the things I've done for you over the years? Alone, I might add."

She couldn't help it this time. Cynthia rolled her eyes and shook her head. "It isn't my fault you're alone. Don't blame that on me. You're the one who ran off my father."

As soon as the words were out of her mouth, Cynthia knew her mistake.

Cybil's face took on a cold, flat expression. She put down her footrest and stood up. "I'm going to bed." She brushed past Cynthia.

"Mom," Cynthia called after her, "what about dessert?"

Her mother stopped but didn't turn around. "You eat it. You're already fat. An extra dessert won't matter." She looked over her shoulder and added, "And since that's how you feel about me, you need to be out of this house before I get home from work tomorrow. I have a pottery studio to build."

Chapter 9

The rest of the evening was a blur as Cynthia made frantic phone calls. No one in town had a guest room to spare. She couldn't afford a motel room for more than a few days. Faced with homelessness, she gave in and called Mrs. Andrews about the room over her garage.

"Of course you can have it. In fact, I cleaned it out this week, so it's ready. When do you want to move in?"

"Is tomorrow too soon?" asked Cynthia. She didn't know how much the rent would be, but she would cross that bridge when she came to it. "I don't mean to rush you, but I'm in a bind."

"Cybil really wants to get started on that pottery studio, huh?"

"Something like that." Everyone in town would find out she'd been kicked out of the house, but Cynthia wasn't going to be the source of that information. "I can be there first thing in the morning to sign the contract, and I don't have much stuff, so moving shouldn't take long."

"I'll email the contract now to save time. The apartment is fully furnished. Is that okay?"

Cynthia looked around her room at the twin bed, nightstand, dresser, and desk from her childhood. Her mother hadn't specified anything about taking or leaving furniture. Leaving it behind would be easier for Cynthia, but that left more work for her mother. She shook her head. That wasn't her problem anymore.

"That's great. I'll sign the contract tonight. Can I drop things off before work?"

"I'm up at six. I'll have the coffee on."

Cynthia spent the rest of the evening preparing for her move. The contract was straightforward and the rent was reasonable, although at this point she'd have paid anything.

Packing up her possessions didn't take long. She didn't have much since her mother refused to let her use any space outside of her bedroom. Her clothes fit in her suitcases, and she scrounged up a couple boxes from the garage for everything else.

By ten o'clock, the room was bare except for the sheets on the bed, which she planned to throw into a box in the morning. She did her nighttime routine, then threw herself down for the last time on her childhood mattress. It sank and creaked under her weight, but instead of irritating her, it heralded the start of something new.

She thought she'd fall asleep from the stress and exhaustion of the evening, but as soon as she hit the bed, Mark's image popped into her head. She needed to come up with a plan for when she ran into him at Mrs. Andrews' house.

He had to be married by now, didn't he? Cynthia didn't remember seeing an announcement in the *Gazette*. That would have been impossible to miss. And nothing newsworthy in Glen Valley stayed quiet for long, especially when it was about someone whom everyone liked.

Staring at the ceiling, she considered how she would greet him when he came to visit his mother. He didn't visit often. But the thought of seeing him put butterflies in her stomach.

The bedroom door flung open, and Cynthia rolled to her

side in time to see her mother stomp in. Cybil's mouth opened, probably to continue the tirade she'd started earlier in the evening, but it snapped closed again when her eyes connected with the boxes. She turned around in a circle, studying the bare walls and suitcases.

"What is going on?"

Cynthia sat up. "I found somewhere else to live, per your request. You're welcome."

Cybil put her hands on her hips and glared at her. "It took thirty-five years and now you're listening. It's a miracle. Where do you think you're going?"

"Mary Beth Andrews' house. I'll be gone before you get up in the morning."

Her mother paced around the room, checking the boxes and nudging the suitcases. She opened the closet doors, running her finger across the bare wire hangers. The twinkling noise echoed in the empty closet. Next, Cybil pulled open the dresser drawers, then slammed them closed.

"What about my grade book? Or the fact that it's your turn to cook dinner this weekend? I suppose you think this lets you off the hook for your responsibilities."

Cynthia's head throbbed, and she pinched the bridge of her nose. "Mom, you said I had to move out by five tomorrow. If I don't live here, how is any of that my responsibility?"

Cybil threw her arms in the air. "Typical. You give a person an inch and they take a mile. This move is a long time coming, but that doesn't change the fact that you owe me for all the things I've done over the years. You haven't come close to paying me back."

The lack of logic perplexed but didn't surprise Cynthia. Her mother wanted everything her way and didn't care about anyone else's feelings. Cynthia knew this, and it wasn't going to change. But Cynthia also knew that if she didn't acquiesce to her mother now, she might not get any sleep.

"Fine. But this weekend's dinner will be my last. I'll fix the grades this time, but you'll have to get someone in the IT department to teach you how the system works. I won't do it anymore."

"Mary Beth's place is three minutes from here. You have no social life, and your job isn't that demanding. Nothing goes on in town, anyway." She pulled a push pin out of the wall and threw it in the trash. "How you ever won another award is beyond me. Oh, and next time you win something, let me know. Eveline embarrassed me at Betty's yesterday. Why should she know more about my daughter than I do?"

Cynthia sat up and glared at her mother. "She cares enough to ask." Cynthia knew that wasn't true. Eveline loved to dangle tidbits of information in front of anyone she thought she could get a rise from, and Cybil always fell for it. "Although I didn't tell her."

"Right. As if someone else knew about that stupid contest."

Cynthia ground her teeth together to keep from responding. Helene or Betty must have told Eveline, but Cynthia knew better than to point that out. Cybil didn't take correction well.

"And what's this I hear about you getting your eggs harvested for a story idea? That's a bit much, if you ask me."

Cynthia finally snapped. "I *didn't* ask, and your opinion isn't wanted or needed. Now, could you please leave? I've had a long night and I need to move my stuff to Mrs. Andrews' house before work tomorrow."

Cybil's cheeks paled. "Young lady, I am still your mother, and you need to be respectful. Telling me what to do is nothing of the sort, and we need to discuss this egg thing. You don't know anything about your father. How do you know your eggs are any good?"

Cynthia didn't have the energy for this fight, so she pointed at the door. "Please leave. I'll be gone tomorrow, and you won't have to worry about my articles or the viability of my eggs after that."

Cybil stomped her foot. "Your behavior reflects on me. What will people say when they hear you're trading in your fertility for an award? I might not be able to go to Bunco after this. Don't you care if people judge me because of how you act?"

"Enough!" Cynthia's voice came out harsher than she intended, but she didn't care anymore. "I don't care who judges you. I'm doing what I need to do."

Cybil's jaw tightened, a sign Cynthia recognized well. Cybil's feelings were hurt, and there would be no further conversation until Cynthia apologized—which she didn't intend to do anytime soon.

Her mother turned and left the room, closing the door quietly behind her. The passive-aggressive behavior was typical, but Cynthia didn't plan to be around for the tirade that came in the morning. She hopped out of bed and pushed the boxes against the door in case her mother decided to pay her another visit, then fell back into bed where exhaustion took her, and she fell asleep.

Chapter 10

By the time she got to the office the next day, Cynthia's belongings were tucked away in her new apartment, and she was sipping a large travel mug of freshly brewed coffee and nibbling the best cinnamon roll she'd eaten in years.

Mrs. Andrews had not only welcomed her at 6 a.m., but she also stuck around to help unload and unpack Cynthia's stuff. At first, Cynthia felt awkward about it, but Mary Beth, who insisted on being called by her first name, assured her it was fine.

"Cynthia, I'm thrilled to have someone using this space. It's even more exciting that you're a friend of Mark's. Helping locals is the best feeling. Plus, I can't reorganize my cabinets again, so I might as well help you."

While she was glad to have help, Cynthia wanted to set some boundaries. She didn't want to leave her mother's house only to wind up being mothered by her landlady. But she couldn't resist taking the coffee and roll.

"Where'd you get that?" Dan asked as he poked his head into her office. "I didn't know Betty was bringing treats."

Cynthia smiled and took a bite of the roll. She enjoyed

making Dan wait as she chewed. Just to irritate him, she took a long sip of coffee before replying.

"Brought it from home. This didn't come from Betty's."

Dan moved further into the office and frowned. "Since when did your mother make cinnamon rolls and share them with you?" He pointed at the travel mug. "And she never sends coffee with you. Did someone knock some sense into her?"

Cynthia stifled a laugh. It wasn't funny that everyone knew what her mother was like, but it saved some explanations.

"I moved into the apartment over Mrs. Andrews' garage. Apparently, coffee and cinnamon rolls are part of the lease."

Dan made himself at home in one of her guest chairs. "Well, feel free to bring me coffee and rolls from now on. You can't eat an entire pan of them yourself, and I'm happy to help."

Cynthia glanced at her calendar. "Do we have a meeting this morning?"

Dan stretched out his legs and folded his arms over his lap. "No. Can't I come in and sit without an appointment?"

"You can, but you never do. Whenever you end up in my office, it's because you need me to do something or something's wrong." She enjoyed another sip of coffee before asking, "Which is it?"

"Both. Helene called this morning. Her grandkids have pink eye, and she needs to stay with them. Can you take her appointment with the therapist? Dr. Austen doesn't have another opening for a week, and Helene wanted to get started on the premarital counseling column." He nodded at her computer. "She emailed you the details and her list of questions. I looked over them already. She's got a great angle."

Cynthia pulled up her inbox and skimmed the email. "Works for me. I'll be happy to help on this one, considering Helene came up with my next big break."

Dan shook his head. "You keep saying that, but even if

you win, you don't want to leave me. I'm the best boss you'll ever have."

Their laughter was interrupted by a man's voice.

"Sounds like this is the place to be." Brad Gerome stood in the doorway, a grin on his face and his ever-present leather satchel over his shoulder. "Hope it's okay I came back. Jason said it was fine."

Dan stood up and shook Brad's hand. "Always happy to have you here. What can we do for you?"

Brad nodded toward Cynthia. "Wanted to chat with your award-winning reporter about some wedding venue information. Helene let the cat out of the bag on my next project, so I stopped in to give Cynthia some details in case she wants to write about it. Or if she needs to do some fact-checking."

"I'll get out of your way." Dan clapped Brad on the back and called on his way out, "Cynthia, thanks for taking care of Dr. Austen."

Brad closed the door as soon as Dan left, an indication that the wedding venue project wasn't the only thing he wanted to talk about. It didn't bother Cynthia like it would have if his brother, Doug, had been in the office. Doug closed doors to say horrible things to people; Brad closed doors to spare them embarrassment.

In fact, of all the Geromes, Brad was the only one Cynthia cared for. Brad supported the town's activities and encouraged people to buy local when they could. It might have been because he was the only architect, and his husband was the only chiropractor in town, but Cynthia thought Brad really cared for Glen Valley. Plus, Helene couldn't stop raving about what a great person he was.

Cynthia waved Brad into a chair. "I only have a few minutes before I have to leave for an appointment, but since you closed the door, I'm guessing it's serious."

Brad leaned on the back of the chair. "Not sure it's serious, but I wanted you to hear it from me first: I'm heading to your mom's house this afternoon—she's ready to gut your bedroom and wants me to draw up the plans."

"That didn't take long," Cynthia said. She waited for some sign that the news bothered her—maybe a lump in her throat or a pit in her stomach—but she felt fine. "I moved out this morning. Do you always have appointments available at short notice?"

He cleared his throat. "She made the appointment two weeks ago."

There it was. Her stomach clenched as she put together the pieces. Whatever she had done or not done this past week wouldn't have affected the outcome. Her mother wanted her out of the house and probably even knew about Mrs. Andrews' open apartment. Cybil might have put Betty up to mentioning it, but for some reason, Cynthia doubted Betty had anything to do with it. That would have been a happy coincidence for her mother.

Cynthia shook her head. She may not like her mother much, but she had to give her credit. The woman knew how to manipulate people.

"Thanks for letting me know," she said to Brad. "I absolve you of any guilt. What do you have planned for the space?"

"Are you sure you're okay with this?" Brad slid the satchel from his shoulder and opened it. "As much as I don't want to do it, the project has a lot of potential. I don't get to develop creative spaces like this often."

Brad spread out his drawings on her desk, and, even though the loss of her room was fresh, she could see Brad was right. This was a one-of-a-kind project that didn't come along every day.

"At least something good came out of this," Cynthia said as she helped him stack the drawings. "You're getting a great opportunity to test your skills and implement new things."

"You got something good too," Brad said as he tucked his drawings back into the satchel.

Cynthia frowned. "What's that?"

"You have a new place to live with someone who wants you there. And I know for a fact that Mrs. Andrews makes the best cinnamon rolls in the county."

"Can't argue with that. I may need a new gym membership, too!"

Chapter 11

The drive to Dr. Austen's office was quicker than Cynthia expected. It was outside of Glen Valley, which gave residents a buffer between their therapist and their daily lives, since Dr. Austen was the only family and marriage therapist in three counties.

The trip might have been quicker still because Cynthia had skipped Helene's directions to stop at the local coffee shop that served "the best hazelnut latte ever—*do not* tell Betty I said that," since Mrs. Andrews' brew contained more than enough caffeine for an entire day.

Either way, Cynthia arrived in the waiting room with five minutes to spare. She settled herself onto the brown leather sofa in the waiting area and pulled out the questions Helene had emailed her. She'd been over them several times already and had added a few of her own, but she liked to be prepared. "Over-prepared" was what her mother called it, but Cynthia ignored her. A person didn't win two major journalism awards without putting in the time.

The thought of the award reminded her to check her own schedule. Her first appointment for the egg retrieval process was scheduled for next week, and she wanted to know what was in store. According to her research, she could expect two weeks of hormone injections interspersed with ultrasounds every few days before her body produced enough eggs to be retrieved.

Sinking back into the couch, she sighed. Dan might have had a point when he mentioned the physical wear and tear of the process. Everything she'd read said it was safe, with minimal side effects, but some accounts highlighted the mood swings and the rare but possible blood clots.

She'd also neglected to tell Dan how much work she would be missing. He was all about getting a story, but having to be out of the office for ultrasounds every couple days was sure to drive her editor insane.

Cynthia had no idea what she was going to do when she needed a ride home from the clinic after the retrieval process. The information she'd found said she couldn't drive immediately after the procedure. Maybe she could ask Helene, since she'd taken this appointment as a favor to her.

As Cynthia considered the option, the door to Dr. Austen's office opened, and Eveline Gerome's nasal tone entered the room.

"It just isn't fair, though. Why should people who chose a profession like teaching get handouts? They knew what they were getting into. Besides, Roger and I could have paid for the food, but the PTO beat us to it. Of course, we would have found someplace more upscale than Betty's. . . ."

Cynthia cringed. Arriving early to appointments had its downside. She'd heard Eveline complain, but it always surprised her how short-sighted the woman could be. She ducked her head and studied the schedule in front of her. Maybe Eveline wouldn't see her if she kept still.

"Oh, and speak of the devil, here is her spawn."

Cynthia closed her eyes and made a promise to herself she wouldn't let Eveline antagonize her to the point she needed therapy.

Pasting a smile on her face, Cynthia looked up. "Hello, Mrs. Gerome. How are you today?"

"Hungry." Eveline turned, her fake Birkin bag knocking into a lamp that teetered precariously, and glared at Dr. Austen, who seemed immune to Eveline's wrath. "You really do need a separate exit. Our community is too small, and now this one will be telling everyone in town she saw me in your office. What will people think if someone with my social status is seen in therapy?"

The fake smile on Cynthia's face turned real. Everyone in town already knew Eveline had a standing appointment, but no one said anything. They were waiting to see if it improved her disposition, but so far, nothing had changed. Not that anyone expected it to.

"I'll take that into consideration," Dr. Austen said, and hustled the woman out the door.

Whatever else the therapist said to her patient, Cynthia couldn't hear, but Eveline didn't seem pleased as she gave her trademark hair flick, then slammed the door on her way out. Cynthia watched Dr. Austen's shoulders slouch for a few seconds, then heard her take a deep breath before turning around, a calm and serene facade plastered to her face.

"You can come on back, Cynthia. Helene told me you were sitting in for her today."

Cynthia followed the therapist into her office and took in the surroundings. She could see Eveline's fresh butt imprint on the couch and sat down at the other end.

"You know, if you need some time to decompress after Eveline, I have a few minutes. She can be trying to say the least. If you ever want to get under her skin, ask her why she still wears yoga pants." Cynthia knew she shouldn't gloat, but it was the one time she'd been able to irritate Eveline so much that she didn't have a comeback. "It's petty, but it feels really good."

Cynthia saw the grin on Dr. Austen's lips for a second before the therapist got control of herself.

"Strictly speaking, I can't talk about other patients." She looked up at the ceiling for a second and rotated her head as if she were releasing stress. "But there are some patients who are more trying than others." With that, Dr. Austen grabbed a leather-bound portfolio with the initials *PEA* on the front and opened it. "Now, you're here to go over the marriage counseling material for Helene's column. So, let's do that."

The two of them reviewed Helene's outline, with Cynthia making suggestions and Dr. Austen correcting them both. Cynthia had never worked with someone this organized before; it was a nice change from what she was used to. At one point, she asked the counselor, "Have you considered writing a book? This material is great, and you tell it in a way that everyone could understand."

From the flush of pink in the therapist's cheeks, Cynthia gathered that Dr. Austen might be pleased with her suggestion.

"I've considered it, but writing isn't my strong suit."

Cynthia surprised herself when she offered, "Let me know if you want to pursue it. I'd be happy to help. The process wouldn't be that much different from what we just did; and with all your anecdotes, the article's going to have a nice, easy flow to it. I was going to let Helene write it up, but I think I'm going to instead. I can get it finished before she gets off nursing duty for pink eye."

Dr. Austen nodded. "She'll appreciate that. I can say this without breaking any patient confidentiality, but Helene is so much happier now than when I met her last year. That's one of the joys of my job—seeing the results." She paused and frowned. "Not that it happens with every patient."

Cynthia assumed Dr. Austen was referring to Eveline but didn't comment. Instead, she changed the subject.

"Not sure if Helene mentioned it, but I'm working on a

story about egg harvesting. I'm going to have it done myself so I can give a firsthand account. Have you ever counseled anyone going through the process? Any suggestions?"

Dr. Austen nodded and rubbed her hands together. "What a great topic. Not enough people who go through this or in-vitro fertilization take the time to evaluate and reflect on what is happening. I have an entire course of therapy, plus a list of recommended reading. I'd be happy to give you the list if you want."

"That would be great." Cynthia paused, wondering if Helene would mind when she found out Dr. Austen could help with her piece. "If you have availability, I'd be interested in interviewing you for my story as well."

Clapping excitedly, Dr. Austen grinned. "Pardon my unprofessional enthusiasm, but you've made my day. This type of coverage, both what Helene is doing and what you proposed, is difficult but necessary. Let's talk logistics so we can get things scheduled."

By the time she waved goodbye to Dr. Austen, Cynthia was more excited about this project than she'd been about either of her award-winning stories. She didn't even mind when, on her way back to the office, Cybil called to demand she set up an appointment with the plumber. In fact, she offered to meet the plumber the next day.

This time next year, Cynthia knew she'd be anywhere but Glen Valley.

Chapter 12

"What do you mean, you're coming for a visit?"

Mark Andrews furrowed his brow. His mother usually welcomed his visits. Granted, his last trip home with Jessie, now his ex-girlfriend, had ended poorly, but dismay was the last thing he expected to hear in his mother's voice.

"I've got a long weekend coming up, so I thought I'd come stay in the apartment, and we can go to that farmer's market you like. Or the antique mall in Henrietta. Brunch at Betty's. Whatever you want to do. The entire weekend is yours."

Mark cringed. He sounded as guilty as when he'd used her brand-new, white guest towels to clean mud off his boots when he was ten. His infraction this time wasn't as bad, he hoped.

In the ten months he'd dated Jessie, Mark had only visited Glen Valley once—for his mother's birthday. He'd told her it was because Jessie was more of a city person. She didn't enjoy small-town life at all. The lack of Lululemon, Starbucks, and Whole Foods gave her anxiety.

But the truth was he hadn't wanted to run into Cynthia Anderson again. The hour they'd spent together working on his mother's birthday profile had confirmed his infatuation was alive and well. So, it was easier to make excuses and blame Jessie for not visiting than to tell his mother the truth.

And now his plan seemed to have backfired.

"It's sweet that you want to visit, but what does Jessie think? As I recall, she wasn't a fan of our town. Or me, for that matter."

"We broke up, Mom. I was going to tell you when I got there, but it will just be me."

"Oh. Well, I'm sorry." She paused. "Actually, I'm not. She wasn't a nice girl, if you ask me. But it will be nice to have you visit. Henrietta sounds wonderful, and everyone's raving about Betty's new weekend buffet. It will be lovely to have you home, but you'll have to stay in the house with me. I rented out the apartment."

Mark shook his head. His mother's hesitation made sense now.

"Mom, we agreed that you weren't renting it out anymore. That last tenant was crazy."

"Mark William Andrews, be nice. He wasn't crazy. Randy was just free-spirited."

"Same thing." This was his own fault. If he'd visited more often, he would have known what was going on. "Mom, you don't need the money or the hassle of having someone you don't know living there."

"I know. We've gone over my finances several times. But it isn't a hassle, honey, and this time I've let it to someone I know and who has excellent references. I'm really enjoying the company."

Mark did a mental inventory of possible tenants. He cringed at the first name that popped up.

"Please tell me you didn't rent to Doug Gerome. We've been down that path before, Mom. I know you want to help him, but I think he's beyond hope."

He could hear the irritation in his mother's voice when she answered.

"I would never rent to Doug. Maybe his brother, Brad, but really, the place is too small to start a family. Did I tell you Brad and Carlton want to start a family?"

Mark relaxed. He was glad his mother hadn't fallen prey to Doug's charms again. And while he was happy she wasn't concerned about same-sex marriages, she was still hiding something.

"Yes, Mom. You told me. Can you stop avoiding the question and tell me who's moved in?"

His mother's long pause made him nervous. Something told him he wasn't going to like her answer.

"Now, don't get upset with me, but it's Cynthia Anderson."

Mark concealed his anxiety and asked, "Why didn't you just say so?"

"Because I knew you wouldn't like it, and because Cybil gave her an ultimatum, so she had nowhere else to go. I couldn't let the poor girl go homeless. Anyway, she's doing me a favor. We have breakfast together in the mornings. She loves my coffee, and I'm having so much fun making cinnamon rolls and bear claws and raspberry kolaches to share. It's been wonderful having somebody who enjoys my cooking. You should be happy for me."

He was happy for her. She'd been alone a long time, ever since his dad died. Mark had hoped having renters would keep her company. None of them had ever spent time with her, though. He knew Cynthia really liked his mother or she wouldn't do it.

That wasn't the real issue, though. Mark wondered if his mother knew the truth.

"I won't tell Cynthia you have a crush on her," said his mother.

The shock of the statement kept him quiet.

She continued, "You couldn't stop talking about her in high school. Everything was 'Cynthia likes this' and 'Cynthia said that.' Your dad and I were so surprised you never asked her out."

At the mention of his father, Mark asked, "Dad knew?"

"Of course he did. He wasn't thrilled you fell for Cybil Anderson's daughter, considering her questionable parentage, but Cynthia was nice enough. He always hoped you would figure things out and end up together." Her voice broke when she said, "We talked about it the day before he had the heart attack. I never told you that, but maybe I should have. It would have saved you from all those other women—Jessie included." She cleared her throat before she continued. "Speaking of which, make sure the next girl you date likes small towns. I've really missed you."

Promising himself he would never judge someone for who her parents were, he asked, "Why did Cynthia move out of her mother's house?"

"Cybil is turning Cynthia's bedroom into a pottery studio."

"Last time we talked, you said Cynthia had a few more months before she had to be out."

"I did, but for some reason, Cybil changed her mind. Cynthia called me on a Thursday night and moved in the next morning. The gossip tree hasn't found out the real reason, and I haven't wanted to bother Cynthia about it."

"Cybil isn't known for her rational behavior," Mark conceded. "Remember when I had her as a third-grade teacher? The grading scale depended on her mood of the day."

Mrs. Andrews clucked at her son. "You be nice. Cybil's had a lot on her plate. She was a single, working mom before it became a commonplace thing." She changed the subject. "Let's talk about what dates you'll be here. I can't wait to show you off to Glen Valley."

He didn't have time to worry about Cynthia anymore as they planned his visit.

"I think we should hit all the farmer's markets in the area, plus the antique malls. You have a lot of catching up to do," she said.

That's when he knew she wasn't mad at him. Now all he had to figure out was how he was going to avoid Cynthia. But he decided to worry about that another day. He needed to pay attention to the conversation with his mother, or he would need to rent a trailer to bring all her anticipated purchases home.

Chapter 13

Less than two weeks after her second journalism win, Cynthia found herself in the fertility doctor's office, which couldn't have been more different from Dr. Austen's. The clinical white of the waiting room walls did nothing to ease her trepidation. It also didn't help that Cynthia was sitting alone in an otherwise couple-filled room.

Most of the women flipped through outdated magazines while the men stared at the television that blared out the morning talk show. Cynthia had imagined the office would be bright and cheery, but even the chair she sat on felt unwelcoming, hard, and lumpy. An article she once read had suggested that comfortable waiting rooms made for happier patients. Maybe she should find the study and give it to the doctor.

"Cynthia Anderson?"

A nurse called her name, and she stood up. Several pairs of eyes followed her as she walked across the room, and she noticed one woman lean over to her husband and whispered in his ear.

Knowing she was being oversensitive, Cynthia followed the nurse and ignored her feelings. No one cared that a single woman was at a fertility clinic. It was the twenty-first century, wasn't it?

The intake questions were simple, although she noticed she'd gained a few pounds from Mrs. Andrews' fresh pastries. The nurse reviewed the questionnaire she'd completed, and everything went smoothly until Cynthia mentioned she was a reporter and planned to document the procedures for the *Gazette.*

"I doubt the doctor will approve that," grunted the nurse.

"I'm not naming the clinic. It's more of an inside perspective of what it takes to go through the process. My focus is on the emotional and physiological toll of hormone injections as well as the procedure itself." That wasn't exactly what Cynthia had planned, but she knew from experience it paid to keep some cards close to her chest. "Besides, I explained all this on the phone when I made the appointment."

The nurse looked down at Cynthia over her glasses. "I hope someone shared it with the doctor, then, and that he's in a good mood today. Otherwise, you've wasted everyone's time." Without another word, she stomped out of the exam room.

Cynthia's nerves kicked in, and she wondered what had just happened. Everything had been cleared through the appropriate legal departments. She pulled her phone out of her purse and sent a text to Dan.

Did you get the consent form from Dr. Purdue?

The reply was instant. *Yes. Why?*

She didn't want to raise an alarm if nothing was wrong, but it was good to know things were in her favor.

Just checking. Waiting on doctor.

Someone knocked on the door before Dan replied. She dropped the phone into her purse and called out, "Come in."

"Hello. I'm Dr. Purdue." The man's face was buried in the paperwork he was holding, so all she could see was the bald spot on top of his head. "Says here you're interested in having your eggs harvested. File says you're healthy; a little heavier than is ideal."

The insult irritated her, and she let loose.

"Is that how you greet all your new patients? Tact might work a little better, if you ask me."

The doctor's head whipped up. She thought he looked surprised that someone would question him, and she soon found out she was right.

"So, you're the reporter I've heard so much about. Dan warned me you could be surly."

Planning a vicious string of insults for Dan when she got back to the office, she concentrated on the issue at hand. "Not surly as much as proactive. I stand up for myself. While you might be right about my weight and age, that isn't the best way to start a conversation with someone who's getting ready to shell out tens of thousands of dollars for a procedure that may or may not work."

The doctor chuckled as he pulled out a stool and sat down. "Truce, then. Judi said you were wound up tight, and Dan gave me permission to mess with you." He held out his hand. "Let's start again. I'm Dr. Purdue. You are Cynthia Anderson, and you're here to write a story that will launch you into the big leagues. Nice to meet you."

"How do you know Dan?" she asked as she shook his hand. "He didn't mention anything."

"Old friend. We caught up when he submitted the consent forms. I usually wouldn't do something like this, but I stole his girlfriend in the seventh grade. Figure I owe him. Now, let's get this examination started."

The remainder of the appointment was straightforward. Dr. Purdue reviewed routine test results, explained the hormone injection protocol and its side effects, and reminded her she needed a ride home the day of egg retrieval.

"I can drive myself. I'm only twenty minutes from here," said Cynthia. "No need to bother anyone."

Dr. Purdue shook his head. "You aren't allowed to drive. The procedure requires sedation, and we want someone to monitor you for the first few hours afterwards. This is non-negotiable. You show up alone on retrieval day and I won't do it. Trust me—it's for your own good."

Cynthia agreed. Helene would help since this was her idea. If she didn't have time, Mrs. Andrews would be a good backup option. Her landlady was always asking what she could do to help. This would be perfect.

"Any other questions you have for me? If not, I'll see you Monday for the first screening."

Cynthia glanced at her list and noticed one item she'd forgotten. "Genetic testing. I read some articles that it might be a good time to get the basic testing done so that when"—she paused for effect—"or *if* I decide to use the eggs, I'll be able to get a better match from the sperm bank."

Dr. Purdue nodded. "I don't recommend it for a variety of reasons, but I can put in an order. The lab next door offers a standard set of tests to see what genetic disorders, if any, you carry. It's not a guarantee we'll catch everything, but you can find out about various cancers, mitochondrial disorders, cystic fibrosis . . . I can write the orders if you want."

"Yes, please."

Genetic testing would make for a good ancillary article that could turn into a feature story at some point. The article wouldn't be about her but more about the process and what it could mean for families with genetic disorders.

Cynthia wouldn't look at her own results. The logical part of her knew she should. She didn't know her father, and these tests might tell her something that could save her own life somewhere down the road. But it might also tell her something she didn't want to know.

For now, she was doing this for the story and the story alone. That was enough.

Chapter 14

Cynthia ran her hands through her hair in frustration. She had never considered how controversial egg harvesting was. She thought her mother's comment was a one-off, but instead, her research revealed that it was a hot button for many groups. Caution needed to be used when she wrote the article. Dan wanted fair coverage for all sides of any issue, but the readers of the *Gazette* were conservative to say the least. The last thing Cynthia wanted to do was cause people to cancel their newspaper subscriptions.

She shifted in her seat and winced. Her butt was a pincushion. A week into the hormone injection process and she was already tired of it. The doctor had warned her she might need help, but she had no one to ask. Every injection was a test of her flexibility, aiming to target an unpunctured spot on her bottom or the backs of her thighs. If she weren't doing a story on this, she might be tempted to throw in the towel, but this would get her out of Glen Valley.

It had better.

A knock at the door interrupted her thoughts, and she glanced up to see Thomas Radcliffe standing there. Her mother had contracted the relationship coordinator the previous year to find her a husband. So far, she'd had a series of bad dates, not even good enough to write a column about. The agreement expired next month, and she'd been avoiding Thomas's calls.

But she smiled and waved him into her office. "This is a surprise." It wasn't, but she could pretend like the best of them. "What can I do for you?"

"Answer your phone. Then I wouldn't have to drive over here," said Thomas. He went to the window and looked out.

She'd grown used to the amateur ornithologist checking her windows for visiting birds, but she still couldn't join his enthusiasm. Birds carried diseases and, for the life of her, she didn't understand what was so fascinating to watch in the first place.

He pulled his bird-watching journal out of his bag and jotted a few notes before he turned back to her. She was not Thomas's main interest, but he did have to do his job.

"I have a match for you. Can you go on a date Friday?"

The abrupt question left her blinking. "Wow. Didn't see that one coming."

"Frankly, I didn't either. Your less-than-stellar rating has made it virtually impossible to find matches, but I am nothing if not a genius." He pulled a stack of paper out of his bag and tossed it onto the desk. "Henry Livingston the third. He lives two counties over. Accountant. New to the area. Recently divorced. No kids."

Cynthia picked up the papers and glanced at them. Henry stared back at her from the photo with two beady, black eyes barely visible under the fedora sitting haphazardly on his head. This was a vast improvement from Maurice, the butcher from Sun City, whose profile picture had included a meat grinder, but she wasn't sure she had it in her to date one more of Thomas's desperate goons.

She slid the papers back toward Thomas. "I've told you

before—the contract expires soon. Let's just let it expire, and you won't have to deal with me anymore."

Thomas plunked down in her office chair. "About that. Have you talked to your mother lately?"

She glanced down at the stack of messages Jason had delivered but she hadn't read. Ignoring her mother seemed like the easiest thing in the world.

"No. I have not. And I'm not going to."

"That might be a mistake. She renewed the contract."

"What?" Cynthia stood up and went around her desk. "How can she do that? Why did you let her do that?"

Thomas shrugged. "That's how I make money." He held up his hand. "I know you don't want to do this, but there are only so many single women in the area. And Cybil and Helene are the only two mothers who have gifted their daughters with a dating service. Now that both Sara and Tasha are spoken for, you have all the men to yourself. You're my priority client going forward. I committed to ten dates."

Cynthia paced around her office. "Ten? That's more than I had all last year. And most of them were horrible. Isn't that enough torture?"

"Apparently not. And, to be fair, they weren't all bad dates. If I recall, you did enjoy a couple. Remember how you raved about the curling lessons? And you won the hokey pokey when you went roller skating. That was fun, right?"

She tapped her fingers against the window and watched as a bird, though she didn't know what kind, flew away.

"It was fun. But did you notice something?"

Thomas shook his head.

"You knew which activities I liked but didn't mention who they were with," she pressed. "Why is that?"

"Because you didn't like the date, only the activity."

"Correct. That should tell you something."

He tucked his journal back into his bag and stood up. "Look, I'm going to fulfill my end of the deal. If you don't go on the dates, that's your business." Thomas gave her shoulder a pat. "Call Henry if you don't want to meet him at the Pizza Palace tomorrow at five."

"That's kinda early for a Friday, don't you think?"

Thomas shrugged. "He has a coupon that's only good before five thirty."

Cynthia wanted to throw something at Thomas, but she knew he was only the messenger.

"At least Pizza Palace has good food. Are we doing something fun after dinner, at least?"

Thomas scooted to the door. "The Alfred Hitchcock Extravaganza is showing at the drive-in. He has a coupon for that, too. Have fun," he said as he hurried out the door.

Cynthia collapsed into her chair, considering her options. She could blow off the date, but she didn't have anything else planned. Research for her article was never-ending, but she knew she needed to step away from it for a while to get some clarity. Her mother hadn't called since she'd arranged for the plumber to change out the faucet in the bathroom. Brad was keeping her updated on the status of the pottery studio renovation, but that was going slow, too, thanks to the building permits. She could go for a run, but she didn't like to sweat. She'd never developed any other hobbies since she'd never had time.

No. She'd suck it up and go on the date. The pizza would be good, and you couldn't go wrong with *The Birds* or *Rear Window*. As long as Henry didn't think she was "the one," things should be fine.

Chapter 15

Her alarm sounded, and Cynthia stretched her arms over her head before she reached over to turn it off. She flopped back in bed and stared at the ceiling. Since moving, she'd slept better than she had in years. She wasn't sure if it was because there was no chance her mother would come barging in or because the queen-size bed Mrs. Andrews had provided was more comfortable than her old twin.

Either way, she was in heaven.

Unlike last night. Her date with Henry to the Hitchcock Movie Extravaganza could have been worse . . . if she'd rolled in honey and laid down on a fire-ant hill.

She sat up and touched her toes, ignoring the injection bruises on her legs.

Henry had talked incessantly about his ex-wife and how this was the first time in ten years he'd been on a date. She'd assumed he would stop talking during the movie, but no such luck. The first film reminded him of the parakeet he'd gifted his wife on their first anniversary. Later, he'd lamented about the time she'd broken her leg and was housebound. The similarities between his life and the movies were creepy, and Cynthia wondered if he was making things up to make himself seem more interesting. Before the third movie started, she'd made up an excuse to leave and caught a ride share back home. She didn't want to know if the forty-five-second shower scene in *Psycho* reminded him of his ex-wife.

With nothing else to do on a Saturday morning, Cynthia decided to walk off some of the pizza from the night before and then do her chores and laundry.

As she stepped off the last step from her apartment, the side door of the main house opened, and her landlady stepped out.

"Good morning, Cynthia. What a beautiful day." Mrs. Andrews held a walking stick in one hand, and a fanny pack was positioned on her waist. "I'm off for my morning walk. Are you heading into the office again? It is the weekend, you know. You're allowed a few days off."

Cynthia smiled. Mrs. Andrews reminded her every time they met that there were other things in life besides work. She appreciated the woman's concern but had explained several times that work was her life right now.

"Actually, I was going for a walk as well. Mind if I join you?" Part of her wanted to be alone, but she'd come to enjoy talking to her landlady over the last few weeks. She refused to believe it had anything to do with the possibility she'd learn anything about Mark and his girlfriend. So far, the only thing Mrs. Andrews had shared about him was that he would be visiting soon. Cynthia didn't know if Jessie was coming, but she couldn't bring herself to ask. "If not, that's okay. I can go the other direction."

"Oh, please. Walking is fine, but walking *with* someone is better." She took Cynthia's elbow and drew her out to the sidewalk. "At least that's what my husband used to say."

A few minutes later, Mrs. Andrews dropped her arm and said, "Martin loved to walk. That was his favorite thing to do in the evening. After Mark moved away to college, we'd make dinner together and then take a stroll around the neighborhood before we did the dishes. It seemed irresponsible when we first started the tradition. I'd always been one to get the kitchen cleaned up before doing anything else, but Martin convinced me it was okay to try new things. 'Live a little, Mary Beth,' he used to say." She sighed. "I'm glad we did."

Cynthia squirmed a bit. The nostalgia Mrs. Andrews shared made her uncomfortable because it was something she'd never been exposed to. Her own mother never spoke about the past unless it was to point out Cynthia's failings. But Mrs. Andrews seemed happier after talking about her late husband.

"I'm not sure I'll ever have something like that if my date last night is any indication," said Cynthia.

Mrs. Andrews laughed. "Why do you keep using that dating service? I've heard Mr. Radcliffe is a nice young man, but he has yet to make a connection for anyone in town."

"How do you know about that?" Cynthia asked.

"It's a small town, dear."

They walked on in silence while Cynthia considered her words. She was reading too much into them. There was no way anyone could know how she felt about Mark after all these years. Cynthia had never told anyone, and Mark had never expressed any interest in her. . . .

Unless he'd said something to his mother. Cynthia felt her pulse rate pick up. Now would be as good a time as any to find out if Mark was still dating that woman. If he was, she had nothing to worry about. But she wasn't sure how to bring it up without being obvious.

They continued in silence until Cynthia saw a yard sign that gave her the perfect chance to ask about Mark.

"Are you going to the antique fair with Mark when he's in town?" She glanced at Mrs. Andrews to see her response.

"Mmm, that's the plan."

Cynthia waited to see if Mrs. Andrews would continue, but after a while, she realized it might be simpler to ask outright. It wasn't like Mrs. Andrews knew she had feelings for Mark.

Before she could ask, though, Mrs. Andrews cleared her throat. "Would you like to join us?"

"I wouldn't want to intrude. You don't get to see him often."

"No. In fact, this is the first time in almost a year that he'll be in town."

"So why would you want to share him with me?"

"Why not? He gets tired of talking to his mother, and you get tired of talking to your old landlady."

"That's not true. I look forward to our conversations. They're more interesting than anything my mother and I used to talk about." She put a hand over her mouth and winced.

"It's okay, dear. Cybil gets on everyone's nerves."

Cynthia sputtered. "Betty mentioned that to me before, but I thought she was just being nice. Mom seems to rub a lot of people the wrong way." She decided now was her chance to get some dirt. "But I don't want to intrude on you and Mark and his girlfriend."

"You won't be intruding, dear. Mark will be happy to see you. And he's on his own this trip."

A shot of excitement ran up Cynthia's back, but she tempered it. Just because the girlfriend wasn't coming didn't mean there wasn't a girlfriend.

"Oh. Does Jessie have to work?"

She realized her mistake when Mrs. Andrews turned and smiled.

"How interesting that you remember his *ex-girlfriend's* name. And before you ask, I don't know why they aren't seeing each other anymore. She didn't strike me as Mark's type. Not like you, anyway."

Cynthia's cheeks felt hot, and she turned away. "What do you mean? I'm not Mark's type. I mean, we're friends. That's all."

"You're right. You and Mark are friends. There was nothing friendly about that woman—not that I would say that to Mark. He and I agreed long ago not to comment on each other's love lives."

That revelation stopped Cynthia in her tracks. "Mark wants you to date?"

Mrs. Andrews threw back her head and let out a laugh louder than Cynthia had imagined her capable. She shook with amusement before she leaned on her cane and took a few deep breaths.

"Yes, he thought I would be lonely after his dad passed, so he set me up on a few dates when I visited his place. They were disastrous, and from then on, we agreed neither of us would offer suggestions unless asked."

"They couldn't have been any worse than the one I was on last night."

"Is that why you were home so early?"

Cynthia's eyes went wide. "Are you keeping tabs on me?"

Mrs. Andrews gave her an innocent look and started walking again. "The headlights shined in my window. I wasn't trying to spy on you. But was it that bad?"

They finished the walk as Cynthia regaled Mrs. Andrews with all the reasons she wouldn't be seeing Henry in the future. As they parted ways at the back door, Cynthia remembered what Dr. Purdue had told her.

"Can I ask you a favor?"

"Yes, I'd be happy to share the blueberry muffins I made today," Mrs. Andrews piped up.

"I'll take those, too, but it's about something else." Cynthia took a steady breath. For some reason, the thought of Mrs. Andrews turning her down bothered her. "I'm sure you've heard that I'm seeing a fertility doctor for egg harvesting. It's for a story, not for personal reasons."

Mrs. Andrews gave her arm a pat. "Yes, dear, I've heard

all about it, and frankly, it's none of my business. You do what is right for you."

"Thank you. But I need someone to drive me home on procedure day and stay with me for a few hours. I planned to ask Helene, but—"

"I'm happy to help. You tell me when you need me and I'm there." She waved a finger at Cynthia. "Now, don't you leave until I get you those muffins."

Cynthia relaxed. One problem down. She'd worry about the extra calories tomorrow.

Chapter 16

"I'm taking off for the weekend," Jason said as he poked his head into Cynthia's office.

She glanced at the clock on her computer and did a double take. It was 11 a.m. on a Tuesday. Jason wasn't known for his work ethic, but this was a stretch even for him.

"Who's covering for you?"

He glanced at the floor and shifted his weight from one foot to another. Cynthia recognized the behavior as Jason's tell: Dan didn't know Jason was leaving.

"I'm not covering," she said. "Go ask Phil."

Jason walked into her office, his palms together, and batted his eyes, which were framed with lashes longer than hers.

"Please. This is a once-in-a-lifetime chance to see RuPaul. The man is iconic. I can't miss this drag show."

Cynthia's eyes grew wide. "RuPaul is coming to Glen Valley? Why didn't I know about this?"

Jason cleared his throat. "It isn't exactly Glen Valley."

Cynthia hated it when Jason avoided questions. "Where exactly is he?"

"He might be in Las Vegas."

"He *might* be, or he *is*?" Cynthia had done a lot of research for a story in Vegas, but she'd never visited. It irked her that the newspaper's customer service rep would get there before she did.

"He *is*. And I've got tickets, but I have to leave now because I'm driving with a friend."

Cynthia rolled her eyes. "You don't have a driver's license or a car."

"I know, which is why I'm at his mercy. And yours!" Jason dropped to his knees in front of her desk. "Please. Please do this for me, and I'll help you whenever you need anything. I swear. I won't let you down."

She jumped out of her seat and rushed around to him. Taking his arm, she pulled him to his feet. "Get up. Hasn't anyone ever told you not to beg? It makes you look pathetic."

Jason shrugged.

She didn't understand why his behavior didn't embarrass him, but for as long as she'd known him, he did whatever he wanted when he wanted without remorse.

"Are you going to talk to Dan or not?" he asked.

"No, I'm not. This is all you."

"Fine. Then I'm sending Roger Gerome back to your office. You deal with him."

Before she could say anything, Jason walked to the door and whistled. "Mr. Gerome, come on back! Cynthia is ready for you."

She glared at him and raised her chin. "Well played. I'm still not covering for you, though. Deal with Dan yourself."

Cynthia smelled his cologne before Roger Gerome sauntered into her office. If she'd been in a cartoon strip, there would have been a big, green cloud following him. Her eyes watered a bit, and she resisted the urge to pinch her nose.

Jason gave her a wicked smile, then raced out of the office, shutting the door behind him.

"You know, we might be more comfortable in the conference room," Cynthia said as she made a wide berth around Roger. She flung open the door, hoping he didn't realize she was moving it to clear the air in her office. "My office is stuffy."

"This isn't going to take long. My wife is concerned that you're spreading rumors about her. I assured her you would do nothing of the sort, but I thought I'd see for myself."

Cynthia positioned herself so she could breathe the fresh air from the hallway. "Last I checked, I'm not spreading any rumors—about Eveline or anyone else. I have written some well-researched articles, but she's not the subject of any of those."

"You should take this more seriously, young lady. I always said your mother raised you to be too lax."

Her ears perked up. She couldn't remember Roger ever mentioning her mother. Cybil and Roger had always avoided each other like the plague, and Cynthia had never understood why. She'd tried for years to figure out what the animosity was all about, but Cybil refused to talk about him, and Betty didn't know anything.

Maybe today was her lucky day.

She took a step back and held out her hands in surrender. "Mr. Gerome, there's no need to insult me or my mother. Now, if you don't mind, can you tell me exactly what I've done to warrant this visit?"

He shoved his hands in his pockets and walked to the window. "Eveline said you saw her at the therapist's office."

She waited for him to say more. When he remained quiet, she shrugged her shoulders. "And?"

He turned back. "And what?"

"Yes, I saw her. No, I didn't tell anyone." Between Jason and Mr. Gerome, this was not how she wanted to spend her morning, but she did her best to stay calm. "Most of the town sees Dr. Austen these days, so it's not like it's a big deal, anyway."

Roger's shoulders dropped, as if her comment solved his problem.

"That's right. Everyone sees Dr. Austen. Humph." A smile crossed his face, and his hands came out of his pockets. "Well, that does explain things, doesn't it?" A frown slid into the place where the smile had been. "Although it doesn't explain the lack of coverage for the E-Bowlas. My bowling team has won the league championships twice and got a tiny write-up in the *Gazette*. When the Glen Geezers won, they got an entire section. It isn't fair. If you ask me, this newspaper is showing the Geezers favoritism on account of Max Shaw being their captain and his wife working at the newspaper."

The change in subject confused Cynthia. Roger's obsession with bowling was well known, but she'd never seen it first-hand. Interesting, though, how quickly he'd forgotten his wife's concerns.

"I don't write sports features," said Cynthia. "That's up to Phil. He's in the office today if you want to talk to him." She held her breath, hoping her time with Roger was finished.

"No, I don't think I will. I'll catch him some other time. Glad we got the other situation resolved, though."

Without a goodbye, Roger walked past her and nodded at Dan, who was standing in the doorway holding several pink slips of paper in his hand. Dan nodded and watched Roger walk out of the office before he turned to Cynthia.

"What the hell was that all about?"

She went back to her desk and sat down. "I dunno. I'm not sure *he* knows." She pointed at the papers. "Messages for me?"

He shook his head as he handed her the stack. "I can't find Jason, and for some reason, the phones are forwarded to my extension. No one showed me how to transfer calls, so I've been taking messages." The grin that appeared on his face made her nervous. "I'm impressed. Someone has been busy on the dating scene. You planning to write another dating exposé for Thomas? Getting some firsthand experience?"

Confused, she shuffled through the papers and realized all the messages were for her, and they were all prospective dates. Thomas wasn't kidding when he said she was a priority customer.

She needed to tell Thomas to stop giving out her office number.

She wasn't sure if it was the extra hormones coursing through her or the concept that someone actually wanted to go out with her that caused a flush of heat to erupt through her body.

"This is odd," she said as she lined up the slips up on her desk.

"You're telling me. How long has it been since you went on a date?"

Cynthia sneered at him. "Four days ago."

"A good date?"

She closed her eyes. "Two years."

"Like I said." Dan looked over his shoulder. "Now that we have that straightened out, do you know where Jason is?"

"He went to a RuPaul drag show."

Dan didn't blink an eye when he said, "Then you're on phone duty," and left her office.

The timing on these calls wasn't great. Should she really be dating someone new when she was about to have her eggs sucked out of her? It never ceased to amaze her that when you wanted something to happen, it never did, but as soon as you moved on, the flood gates opened.

She sighed and picked up the phone. She owed it to Thomas and herself to go out on a few more dates. What was the worst that could happen?

Chapter 17

Turned out the worst thing that could happen was scheduling dates around every-other-day doctor appointments.

"Why did I think now was a good time to harvest my eggs?" she asked the nurse.

This might not have been the best time to ask, while she was dressed in a scratchy cotton gown, lying on her back with her legs in stirrups, and a cold ultrasound wand investigating her nether region, but the nurse was unfazed.

"It's a bit late to change your mind." She pointed at the screen. "See? There're several eggs progressing nicely."

"Oh. That's good. But what I meant was I have five dates lined up in the next three days."

This did get the nurse's attention. "You do know the rules about sex during this process, right?"

Cynthia nodded. "These are all first dates, so no problem there."

The nurse's eyebrows raised. "You'd be surprised." She removed the wand and handed Cynthia some tissues. "All finished. I'll see you Friday for another scan. And remember—"

"I know. No sex. Don't worry about it."

"Again, you'd be surprised," the nurse called over her shoulder as she left the room.

Cynthia discarded the gown, making a mental note to research why all medical garments were uncomfortable, and got dressed.

Today's first date was a lunch at Betty's Coffee Bar. She glanced at the clock on the wall and saw she was going to be right on time. After scheduling her next appointment, she headed to the parking lot and was surprised when she ran into Brad and Carlton.

She greeted them with a wave and then frowned. She didn't know what the social norm was when meeting someone outside a fertility clinic. Should she ask why they were there or wish them a good day and move on?

Carlton saved her from the decision.

"Good morning! I'll spare you the awkwardness. Helene gushed about your investigative project and said we had to meet with the doctor as well. Apparently, he's an advocate for same-sex couples starting a family. So here we are."

"That's wonderful news." Cynthia remembered Helene mentioning the trouble the couple had had finding a surrogate. "I hope Dr. Purdue can help."

"So do we."

Brad looked at Carlton, who gave a slight nod.

Cynthia suspected she knew what was coming next.

"Have you talked to your mother lately?" he asked.

Her good mood bottomed out. "Only about some computer issues and to call a plumber. We don't spend a lot of time chatting."

Carlton's eyebrows raised, but Brad put his hand on his partner's arm. "I'll get us checked in while you and Cynthia talk, okay?"

Cynthia classified Carlton's smile as sympathetic, and she went on alert. Turning to Brad, she asked, "What's going on now?"

"For some reason, Cybil's decided not to put in the studio. The wedding venue is carving out some space for her."

That was the last thing Cynthia expected to hear, and she wasn't sure what to say. "Okay. It's odd, but it's her decision."

"I should let her talk to you, but I got the impression she misses you. She wants you to move back home."

"That's the craziest thing I've ever heard. Why would I do that?" Cynthia thought about her new apartment and shrugged. "I love where I am now. There's no reason to go back."

"I thought the same, but I just wanted to give you the heads-up." He looked toward the office. "What is Dr. Purdue really like? Helene thinks he's the bee's knees."

She laughed at the antiquated saying, not because it was funny or she was amused but because, if she didn't, she knew she would burst into tears. Her mother was always trying to control her, and it hadn't stopped even when she was out of the house.

"He's fine. The gowns are horrible, but you won't have to worry about that." She glanced at her watch. "Hey, thanks for keeping me updated, but I have to run. I've got a date."

"Helene told me about that, too. Hope it goes well. You deserve it."

She watched him walk into the office before she headed to her car. As she started it up, Cynthia wondered what she should do about the news. Her mother didn't give up on dreams, and the pottery studio had been one for a long time. There had to be a reason she'd changed her mind.

The drive to Betty's didn't yield any answers to her question, and she pushed it out of her head during her lunch with Grady, the IT consultant. Turned out he was only in Glen Valley for a week on a temporary assignment, so she wouldn't pursue a second date, but she had a great time listening to his stories about growing up playing football with his three sisters.

"Once I got to high school, it got easier. Guys don't tackle as hard as girls."

She bid him farewell after lunch and was on her way out when Betty called her back.

"That seemed to go well," said the coffee shop owner. "Was it my German potato salad or your sparkling personality?"

"A little of both, I think. He said he was coming back for lunch tomorrow."

"So, you're seeing him again."

"No. The dating coordinator is setting me up on a bunch of dates and lunches. My mother renewed the contract, and Thomas appeases her."

"Cybil's been on a terror lately. Brad was in yesterday and told me about the change with the studio."

Cynthia nodded, waiting for Betty to add more details, but she didn't.

Instead, Betty asked, "Where do you suppose Thomas is finding all these men? He had nothing all last year, and now you've had two dates in less than a week."

"Thanks for the reminder about my less-than-stellar love life," she said. "And on that note, I need to get back to work."

"That's not what I meant, and you know it." Betty pushed a white bakery bag into Cynthia's hand. "Test these out and report back. The new baker at the wedding venue wanted feedback, and I can't eat another slice of cake."

Cynthia saved the cake for her afternoon date. Leonard, the new substitute teacher at the high school, met her promptly in the park at four and was thrilled to have an assignment.

"Does she want a written review of my thoughts, or can I tell you?" he asked as they settled down on a park bench.

Cynthia bit her lip, not understanding why Leonard—not Leo—would take cake tasting so seriously on a first date.

Leonard didn't wait for her response as he took his phone

out of his pocket and photographed each slice before he took minuscule bites and made notes on them.

"What do you think?" she asked after he'd sampled each slice three times.

"The almond with raspberry filling is a bit dry. I'm usually partial to chocolate, but this one is so sweet, it's off-putting. The winner is the vanilla with hazelnut cream." He held out the bag where he'd arranged all the samples. "You should try some."

"I'll pass," Cynthia said, not bothering to explain she had no desire to eat something he'd been nibbling.

Luckily, Leonard didn't press the issue and offered to take his feedback directly to Betty, which freed Cynthia to return to work. Dealing with Dan or Phil seemed like a better way to pass her time than watching this man eat cake.

Chapter 18

The next day, Cynthia made it through dates three and four without any cake or note-taking. Neither was as good as her lunch with Grady, nor as bad as the time with Leonard. She had one more date scheduled that evening, and then she told Thomas she needed a couple days off.

"But I have three more men interested in going out with you."

"I have plans this weekend, and I need some time to reflect. Plus, Dan is cranky about me missing work."

She was glad she was having this conversation over the phone. There were no plans and nothing to reflect on, but despite the fact he'd agreed to a hastily-pitched story idea about the dating service, Dan's patience was wearing thin.

"Fine. But starting Monday, it's game on," said Thomas.

Rolling her eyes, she secretly hoped her eggs would be ready to be retrieved on Monday and she would have one more day of reprieve. Cynthia thanked Thomas and went back to researching the advances in egg harvesting over the years.

She was back in the zone when a knock on the door startled her.

"Sorry to bother you at work," said Mrs. Andrews, "but I missed you this morning."

Cynthia jumped out of her chair to greet her landlady. Her breakfast date had wanted to meet at seven o'clock in the café one county over, so she'd been out of the house at six thirty.

"Early start today. Is everything okay?" Cynthia asked.

Mrs. Andrews took the seat that Cynthia pointed to and nodded. "Oh yes. I just got used to seeing you in the morning, so I wanted to check in on you." She held out a bag. "I made cinnamon streusel coffee cake."

Cynthia held back a groan. All she'd been doing this week was eating, but she knew she wouldn't be able to resist this treat.

"Thank you. Would you like a coffee or anything? I have a few minutes."

"No, that's okay." But Mrs. Andrews made no move to stand up, and her normally cheerful expression was sour. "I did want to ask you something."

"Okay. What's up?"

"I heard from Betty that Cybil wants you to move back in with her."

"That rumor is making its way around town faster than usual." That explained the real purpose of the trip. While Cynthia appreciated the food, this made more sense. "But it is just a rumor. I haven't talked to Mom. Even if she asks me, I'm happy where I am."

Mrs. Andrews's face relaxed, and her cheeks turned rosy. "Thank goodness. I would hate to lose you as a tenant."

Cynthia didn't know what to make of the sentiment. She'd lived in the apartment less than a month, and she didn't spend *that* much time with her landlady. Cynthia chalked it up to the widow's loneliness and went on with her day.

By the time she left for her final date of the week, Cynthia had forgotten about the odd conversation with Mrs. Andrews and made her way back to the Pizza Palace. Living in a small town meant there weren't a lot of dining options available. And Nick, the man she was meeting for dinner, had no idea this was her second time eating there in less than a week.

It turned out Nick wasn't a huge fan of pizza, so the two of them dined on salad and pasta.

"What brings you to Glen Valley?" Cynthia asked. Thomas hadn't given her any information about Nick other than the fact that he wasn't from the area.

"I'm in construction. There're some new commercial buildings going up north of town. I'll be overseeing them."

"The wedding venue?"

He paused with a forkful of lettuce on its way to his lips. "Yeah. How do you know about it?"

"Small town, remember?" She decided he might as well know the full story. "I also know the people spearheading the project. The newspaper will do a story at some point."

A twisted grin lit up his face. "You're the one who suggested the moat, aren't you?"

"Guilty as charged."

"Do you have any idea how long it took to explain why that couldn't happen? It's a cool idea but completely out of scope for the timeframe and budget."

"Honestly, I was being funny. But you must be careful around Helene. She can take things pretty seriously sometimes."

"Not as seriously as Cybil Anderson. That woman is wound tight." His pupils dilated slightly. "Wait. Anderson. Is she related to you? I didn't mean anything—"

"No, you're right. She's one of a kind. And yes, she's my mother."

The rest of the conversation skirted around Cybil and the wedding venue. By the time the check came, Cynthia assumed this would be the one and only time she and Nick went out, but he surprised her.

"I had a great time. Would you like to go out again? Maybe somewhere outside Glen Valley? There's an awesome steak house in Doxberry."

She did some quick mental calculations. If she went out with Nick again, she might be able to avoid the other men Thomas had lined up. Nick entertained her, and even though he'd avoided further discussion about her mother, he hadn't been put off by her either.

"Sure. Let's do it." Her face got warm when she realized what she'd said, but Nick didn't seem to catch the innuendo. They agreed on the following Thursday night, since he would be traveling for a few days, and parted company.

When she got back to her apartment, she noticed Mrs. Andrews's light was still on. She remembered the morning visit and decided to stop in.

"Cynthia! What a delight to see you. I baked some oatmeal-raisin cookies and was making some hot chocolate. Would you care to join me?"

"I'll pass. Dinner at the Pizza Palace was filling." She hesitated. "I didn't want to bother you, but are you okay? You seemed like you wanted some company this morning, and I didn't have a lot of time."

Mrs. Andrews stepped out onto the patio and gave her arm a pat. "Everything is fine, dear. Like I said this morning, I wanted to be sure you were staying. When Cybil gets her head set on something, she doesn't stop until she gets it. Sort of like in high school when she and—" She stopped and laughed nervously. "Oh well. You don't want to hear about that. I'm happy you're staying. How was your date tonight? I assume it was a date. I would hate to be presumptuous."

Cynthia wondered what her mother had set her mind to in high school, but Mrs. Andrews had clearly avoided the topic, and Cynthia was getting tired. Dating and preparing for egg harvesting took a lot out of a girl.

"It was nice. Nick and I are going out again on Thursday."

Mrs. Andrews nodded and glanced back inside. "I best get back to my mystery show. If I miss too much, I won't be able to figure out 'whodunnit.' Good night."

The door closed before Cynthia could add her good night. As odd as that was, she was too tired to put much thought into it. Tomorrow was her next ultrasound, and she needed to edit Helene's latest column before she went to bed. She wasn't looking forward to reading the article "What to Wear on Your Wedding Night," but Helene knew what she was doing. It seemed women wanted tips on everything, including what color negligee would drive their men wild.

If Cynthia ever got married, she planned to stick to her plaid flannel sleep pants and worn-out Glen Valley Vultures T-shirt. There wasn't anything in the world more comfortable.

Chapter 19

The ultrasound the next morning was anything but comfortable. Something was different from two days ago, but the nurse didn't seem concerned.

"You're ready."

"Ready for what?"

Shaking her head, the nurse said, "Ready for egg harvesting. What else would I be talking about? We'll get you scheduled for tomorrow. The 6:00 a.m. appointment is the best time slot because you'll have the whole day to relax afterward."

Cynthia did a double take. Anything earlier than ten on a Saturday was insane. "Tomorrow is Saturday. Can't this wait until Monday?"

"Absolutely not. Your eggs will be perfect tomorrow. If we wait until Monday, we'll miss the window and you'll have to do the entire process over again."

Considering how tired she was of needle pokes, Cynthia nodded. "Okay. Six it is. Should I bring coffee and donuts for everyone?"

The nurse frowned. "Did you *not* read the material we gave you? You can't eat or drink beforehand, remember? And did you get your ride home and someone to stay with you? We can't do this without that person."

"It was a joke!" Cynthia had memorized all the material and knew about the restrictions. She bit her lip. She needed to remember not to joke around this office. "Yes, I have someone. She'll be with me."

The nurse crossed her arms over her chest. "If you show up without a driver, we will turn you away. That is non-negotiable." She tilted her head to the screen. "And all this prep work will be wasted."

Cynthia sat up on the exam table and pulled down the paper gown over her knees. She had no desire to experience this part of the process again, so she planned to stop by Mrs. Andrews's house before going back to work. If, for some reason, tomorrow didn't work for her landlady, she'd call Helene, who would be thrilled to get involved.

▭

CYNTHIA PULLED up in front of Mrs. Andrews's house and frowned. A blue sports car she didn't recognize blocked her spot in the driveway. The last time she'd seen a luxury sports car in town was when Doug Gerome had caused a ruckus at Smith, Rogers & Shaw, the one and only law firm in town.

She licked her lip as she decided whether she should knock or not. No one was in a good mood when Doug was around, but she needed to give Mrs. Andrews a heads-up about the next day.

Preparing herself, she parked the car and ran up to the door. Cynthia started to knock, but Mrs. Andrews pulled it open before her knuckles connected with the wood.

"Did you forget something, dear? You're not usually here during the day."

Cynthia nodded. "Actually, I'm headed back to work after my doctor appointment."

Before she could say more, a voice called from somewhere in the house. A voice she recognized. A voice that still sent shivers down her back.

"Who's at the door, Mom?"

Mechanically, Cynthia smoothed down her hair and straightened her shirt. She wished she'd checked her lipstick in the car's vanity mirror, but it was too late now as she saw Mark step into the hallway.

"Cyn! Nice to see you. Mom said you'd moved into the apartment. How's that working out?"

He leaned in and pulled her into a quick hug. She'd received a few of these when they were in high school, and they never failed to take her breath away. Mark Andrews gave a seriously good hug.

Wishing she could stay in his arms forever, she stepped back reluctantly and said, "It's great. Your mother is a wonderful landlady."

Mrs. Andrews clapped her hands together. "I'm so glad you said that in front of him. He accused me of making things up."

"That isn't what I said." Mark rolled his eyes and put his arm around his mother's shoulders. "Parents. What can you do?"

Cynthia smiled even though she didn't feel the same way about her own mother. She watched enviously as Mrs. Andrews basked in her son's attention, then snapped back to reality when her landlady asked, "What did the doctor say, dear?"

She froze. Chances were Mark already knew the whole story, but how embarrassing to give the details to his mother while he was standing there! Maybe she should call Helene. Or even ask Dan. Technically, this was a work activity. Her boss could give his insight as to how patients' families were treated.

Satisfied with this option, she shook her head. "I don't

want to bother you. Your son's here, and you should enjoy your time with him. It wasn't important."

She turned to leave, but stopped when Mrs. Andrews called out, "Your eggs are ready, aren't they?"

Feeling the heat flood her cheeks, Cynthia turned back around and caught Mark's expression. He seemed confused as he looked back and forth between his mother and her until she saw Mrs. Andrews pat her lower abdomen. Then his mouth dropped open.

"Are you talking about what I think you're talking about?" Mark asked.

Cynthia nodded and put up her hands. "There is a logical explanation, though."

Mrs. Andrews waved her hand. "When do you need help?" She turned and looked at her son. "She needs someone to drive her to the clinic and home again. There is some light sedation when they harvest her eggs."

"Mom!"

Mark's face reminded her of a tomato, and Cynthia relaxed when she realized she wasn't the only person whose mother still had the power to embarrass them.

She backed away from the porch. "I didn't know Mark was in town, so I'll find someone else. It's no problem."

"Absolutely not. Tell me when you need me, and I'll be there."

Cynthia glanced back at Mark, whose cheeks were now more pink than red, and shrugged.

"Check-in time is tomorrow morning at six. I should be ready to go home around eight or so." She rushed to apologize. "It's really early, so if you can't make it, I understand."

"Nonsense. I'm more than happy to help." Mrs. Andrews nodded at Mark. "We aren't going to the antique mall until one, so it works out just fine. Shall we meet in the car at five fifteen? I'll bring the coffee and Danishes."

Relief loosened Cynthia's tight shoulders as she said,

"Thank you. I can't eat beforehand, but the ride will be perfect. I'll get out of your way now." She focused her gaze just over Mark's head and said, "Nice to see you again. Sorry to interrupt your weekend."

Cynthia hurried back to her car. She didn't know if this was the right choice, but she assured herself Mrs. Andrews wouldn't miss any time with Mark. Besides, didn't most people sleep in on vacation, anyway?

Chapter 20

"What's going on?" Mark asked as soon as the front door was closed. "I thought we were spending the weekend together."

He cringed when the words came out of his mouth. He sounded like a petulant toddler instead of an adult child looking out for his mother.

She walked back to the kitchen and opened the refrigerator door. "Cynthia needs a ride to the doctor, and I offered to give her one. We'll have plenty of time." She pulled ingredients out of the refrigerator and put them on the counter. "She needs a hearty meal tomorrow while she rests. I think I'll put together a lasagna."

His mother's words made him realize the two women had been talking about this appointment for a while, especially since his mother only made lasagna on special occasions. On a whim, Mark opened the cabinet door where the lasagna noodles were stored and was greeted with a bag of double-zero flour, the kind his mom only bought when she was making lasagna from scratch. His mother not only knew about this appointment, but she'd also prepared for it.

Grabbing the bag, he put it on the counter next to the eggs, mozzarella cheese, and a mound of Roma tomatoes.

"This feels premeditated if you ask me," Mark said. He leaned back on the counter. "How long have you known this was going to happen?"

"Since Saturday. Helene told me about the feature idea and then Cynthia asked for a ride."

He watched as his mother rinsed the tomatoes and chopped them. "Is that why Cynthia's having her eggs harvested? For a newspaper article?"

That part of the story sounded legitimate, at least. Cynthia had never wanted kids. He remembered in their high school psychology class they'd had to carry around a baby doll for a week to illustrate the responsibility of having a child. Cynthia had failed that section after the teacher discovered she'd stuffed the doll in her locker while interviewing the new principal for the school paper.

"Not that it's any of my business, but you seem to be pretty involved," he pressed.

Mrs. Andrews nodded in time with her chopping motions. "Helene came up with the idea, but she's too old to . . . you know. Cynthia's the perfect age."

"Which is?"

His mother clucked her tongue. "The ideal time to harvest eggs is around thirty-five. Cynthia's a good candidate."

"Why isn't her mom picking her up?"

The glare his mother gave him reminded him of the time he'd thrown a basketball in the kitchen and knocked a full pan of cinnamon rolls onto the floor.

"I retract my question."

She slid the chopped tomatoes into a bowl and added herbs. "Right now, the only thing Cybil has time for is the pottery studio she's opening—which is no longer out of her home but will be at the new wedding venue." She glanced up at him. "Now, I know you have work to do if we're going to make it to the antique mall tomorrow. There will be no telephone calls or texts or stops at the coffee shop to use Wi-Fi. You are mine for one hundred percent of the day tomorrow. Do you understand?"

Mark gave his mother a hug and headed to his laptop. "Yes, Mother. I'll take care of it."

Chapter 21

The next morning, Mark understood that he'd been hoodwinked. His mother shook him awake at 5:00 a.m. to the smell of cinnamon, brown sugar, and coffee.

"It's reheated, but it will get you started this morning so you can get Cynthia to her appointment on time."

"What are you talking about? You agreed to that, not me." He punched his pillow and rolled over. "I'm going back to sleep."

The blanket whooshed off him, and he thanked his lucky stars he'd worn his plaid pajama bottoms to bed.

"Mom! What are you doing?" he asked as he swung his feet to the floor. "I'm not a kid. You can't barge into my room and wake me up like that."

"I'm still your mother. And what I want is to go back to bed because I was up half the night making lasagna and Danishes for today." She exaggerated a yawn as she stretched her arms over her head and pointed to the bathroom. "Make sure you brush your teeth. No one likes morning breath."

Which was how he found himself warming up the car at five fifteen when Cynthia came out of her apartment. The confusion on her face made him smile, which was probably what his mother wanted. He leaned over and opened the door for her.

"Change of plans this morning. Mom's still in bed."

Cynthia leaned down and peered at him. "Is she okay?"

"She's fine." He thought about all the food resting in the refrigerator but decided to fib a bit. "She didn't sleep well last night, that's all. Give her a couple hours and she'll be ready for antiquing."

Cynthia bit her lip, and his heart skipped a beat.

"Are you sure you want to do this? It might be a little awkward," she said.

"I can handle it if you can." He waved her into the car. "Hurry up or we'll be late. Then I'll be in big trouble."

Cynthia slid into the passenger seat without another word and buckled herself in. The car was silent except for the quiet classical music playing in the background. His mother had insisted on classical music.

"It will be relaxing for Cynthia," she'd explained. "She needs to be in a good frame of mind this morning."

When they pulled into the clinic parking lot, Cynthia turned toward him and said, "Thanks for doing this. You don't have to come in. I can have the nurse call you when I'm finished."

Glancing around the quiet lot, he shook his head. "Nothing else to do, and by the time I get home, I'll have to turn right around." He pulled a hardback copy of the latest thriller from the back seat. "Besides, I brought reading material."

She acquiesced without a fight, which was unusual for Cynthia—at least, the Cynthia he knew from high school. He decided she must be nervous and followed her inside.

The waiting room seemed a little cold. He'd hoped for a comfortable chair to read in, but all he saw was a battered couch and lots of straight-backed chairs. The only thing that seemed inviting was the coffee station in the corner, and he promised himself another cup once Cynthia had gotten situated.

"All checked in," she reported. "The nurse said the doctor is on schedule, so this should be pretty quick."

She seemed lost, standing in the waiting room in her gray sweatpants and faded T-shirt with no makeup. Her appearance reminded him of their junior year of high school after she'd lost the debate tournament to Sara Shaw. He couldn't comfort her then, but he could now.

Mark wrapped his arms around her and enveloped her in a hug. "Don't be nervous. This is going to go well for you. I know it." She felt warm in his arms and, without thinking, Mark kissed the top of her head.

The second his lips touched her hair, Cynthia stepped back and blinked at him a few times. She opened her mouth to speak, but the nurse stepped into the waiting room and called her name.

She looked back at him, then shook her head and followed the nurse back for her procedure.

After the door closed behind her, Mark lowered himself slowly onto the couch and dropped his forehead into his palm.

The first thing he planned to do after he got Cynthia safely home was to have a heart-to-heart talk with his mother. This was a matchmaking ploy if he'd ever seen one, and he had fallen for it hook, line, and sinker. It was what he got for being away from home for so long. He'd missed the signs of his mother interfering.

With a sigh, he opened the book he'd brought, but he couldn't concentrate. The look on Cynthia's face after he'd hugged her kept distracting him.

A relationship between the two of them had no future. Sure, he liked Cynthia. He always had. There was no denying that. But it was clear she wasn't ready for a relationship. For pity's sake, she was having her eggs harvested so she could win a stupid journalism award. It wasn't like she wanted a family.

He knew all about her opinions on that subject from high school.

"My mom and I aren't what I would call a family," she'd explained to him years ago. "She raised me and stuff, but I bet I'd get along with my dad better than her."

He cringed when he remembered his response: "You don't even know who your dad is. He could be a convict or the homeless dude that sits outside the car wash in Doxberry." Their math teacher had rushed down the hall, hurrying everyone back to class, and Mark had smirked. "Even worse —*he* could be your dad."

She'd laughed at the comments, but he knew it had bothered her. Cynthia didn't have the connection he had with his mom and dad. Even after his dad died, Mark knew the love and respect they shared was still there. What would it be like to never have a parent love you? And to not know why another parent had abandoned you?

He forced all thoughts of Cynthia out of his head, made himself as comfortable as possible, and focused again on his book. Before he knew what was happening, someone was shaking his arm.

"Mr. Anderson. Wake up. Your wife is finished. She's ready to go home."

He blinked a few times. It took him a few seconds to realize the nurse was talking to him, but for some reason, he didn't mind the mistake. He decided to contemplate it later and focused on the situation. "She's not my wife. I'm just her ride."

The nurse frowned. "Oh. Yeah. She mentioned a friend bringing her in, but I never caught your name. I guess it isn't Mr. Anderson, huh?"

"No. Andrews." Mark shook the sleep from his head and glanced at his watch. He was surprised to see it was almost nine o'clock. "Did everything go okay? She didn't expect to be here this long."

"Everything's fine. It took her a little while to come out of the sedation." The nurse handed him a packet. "Here's the information about the procedure. She can read it and give us a call if she has any questions. Are you the one staying with her today?"

He shrugged. "She didn't mention that. Is she under observation or something?"

"We'd like someone to watch her for the first twenty-four hours to make sure her recovery goes well and there are no complications." She pointed at the packet. "All the details are there. Can you pull the car around back to the procedure exit sign? We'll bring her out to you."

Cynthia didn't look ready to go when she appeared. The nurse steadied her as she walked, catching her when she tripped over the curb. Cynthia's fingers fumbled while opening the car door. Mark started to get out to help, but the nurse shook her head and opened the door herself, then poured Cynthia into the passenger seat.

"Maaaark! What are you doing here?" Cynthia sang as the nurse swiveled her feet into the car. The motion caused her entire body to sway left, and Cynthia's head landed on Mark's shoulder. He looked down to make sure she was okay and was surprised to see her face close to his.

Without warning, she leaned up and kissed him.

He'd always wondered what it would be like to kiss Cynthia Anderson, and even in this awkward situation, he enjoyed the feel of her soft lips on his. It occurred to him that she wouldn't remember the kiss, and he pulled back. He was helping her out today, not making things more complicated.

The nurse cleared her throat. "If you're just a friend, I need more friends like you," she grinned as she settled Cynthia in the seat.

Cynthia flopped like a rag doll, but she slapped away the nurse's hand when she tried to fasten the seat belt. "I can do it."

The nurse gave Mark a curt nod and said, "Good luck with this one," before she shut the car door and went back inside.

Mark watched as Cynthia attempted to fasten the seat belt. She missed the slot four times before he took it from her.

"Feeling pretty good, are you?" Her behavior reminded him of Jessie after she'd had two glasses of champagne, but he kept that thought to himself. "Let's get you settled so you can go home and get back to bed."

She didn't argue, and soon he found out why. Her snores filled the car. He buckled her in and started the car as he remembered the day she'd gotten kicked out of senior government class.

She'd fallen asleep in class and snored—which had happened before, but that time, the teacher thought she was making fun of him. Mark shook his head as he recalled how, the week before, Doug Gerome had recorded the teacher snoring during class and broadcast it over the speaker at a football game.

Even though Cynthia hadn't had anything to do with Doug's prank, the teacher barred her from class for the rest of the week. It made the reason for Cynthia's snoring worse. Mark knew the truth—she'd fought with her mother the night before, and Cybil had locked her out of the house. Cynthia had shivered all night on the front porch, not getting a wink of sleep.

Stuff like this seemed to happen to Cynthia often. Lots of kids—even teachers—thought it was okay to tease her because she was Cybil Anderson's daughter. Cynthia had brushed off the comments, but Mark saw the toll it took on her. With such a cantankerous mother, Cynthia had an uphill battle.

Mark's mother knew it, which explained why he was currently driving her home.

As soon as he turned off the car in the driveway, he watched Cynthia. She'd stopped snoring and looked peaceful, as if she had spent a day on the beach instead of on an operating table.

Mark shuddered. It didn't seem fair that women went through procedures like this when men could father children their entire lives. He knew this was for a news story, but maybe she'd change her mind someday.

He heard a light tap on his car door and turned. His mother stood there, a cup of coffee in her hand. As quietly as possible, he opened the door and reached for the mug.

His mother pulled it back. "This isn't for you. It's for Cynthia. I thought she could use a cup. The appointment went longer than expected."

Mark took the cup from his mother, ignoring her frown, and took a long sip. "She's asleep. You can get her another cup later."

She walked to the other side of the car and peeked in. "How did it go?"

Shrugging, Mark said, "Fine, other than being mistaken for her husband." He kept the subject of the kiss to himself and took another sip of coffee before he broke the news. "Someone needs to stay with her for twenty-four hours. I think we're going to have to push back our plans."

"Oh, don't worry about that. We can go some other time. How often can you take care of an old friend?" She cocked her head. "You can heat up the lasagna when Cynthia wakes up. That would be nice."

The full scope of his mother's deception bloomed in front of him. "You planned this."

With what could only be described as the countenance of an angel, his mother smiled. "How could I plan this? She didn't know until yesterday when the appointment would be. And you just happened to be here." She turned back to her door and called out, "Carry her upstairs. She needs some rest."

Wondering how his mother had managed to pull this off,

Mark unbuckled Cynthia and gently lifted her into his arms. She didn't wake up, but she snuggled close to his chest and tucked her head under his chin. He pushed the door closed with his foot and climbed the stairs. When he reached the top, he paused. Cynthia hadn't brought a purse with her, and he hadn't thought to ask for her apartment key.

Then he saw a pink sticky note on the door that read "You're welcome" in his mother's handwriting. He pushed the door with his foot and, sure enough, it swung open.

"Mom, you have some serious explaining to do," he muttered as he walked inside and tucked Cynthia into bed.

Chapter 22

Cynthia rolled onto her back and stretched. The sun streamed through her bedroom curtains, and the smell of coffee tantalized her nose.

She felt more rested than she had in days. Weeks, actually. The daily injections and hormones must have affected her sleep pattern more than she'd realized. If she was being honest with herself, though, the anxiety and stress leading up to Saturday might be the culprit of her disturbed slumber. Whatever the reason, last night was the best night of sleep she'd had in recent memory.

So good, in fact, she couldn't remember even going to bed.

Sitting up with a start, Cynthia looked around her room. Everything seemed to be where she'd left it when she went downstairs to meet Mrs. Andrews. She swung her legs out of bed and realized she was wearing the same clothes she'd put on for her appointment.

Her eyes widened. She frantically searched her memories. Had she made it to her appointment? What time was it? For that matter, what day was it?

She grabbed for her phone, which she always left on the nightstand, but it wasn't there. She stood up and shuffled out to the living room, where she found Mrs. Andrews on the couch, crocheting.

"I hope you don't mind. You've been in and out since yesterday morning. I thought it best that someone sit here with you." Mrs. Andrews went to the kitchenette and opened the refrigerator. "I stocked your fridge. You need something more than diet soda and jello. What are you hungry for? I made a lasagna, although I'm afraid Mark ate some of it."

At the mention of his name, Cynthia stiffened. Mark had driven her to the clinic, hadn't he? She remembered the drive —at least, she remembered getting in the car. She closed her eyes as she conjured up the ride home, but the only thing she could remember was struggling to buckle her seat belt.

"How're you feeling? The pamphlet said some people have a harder time with sedation than others. Appears you are one of those people."

"Good to know," Cynthia murmured, and winced as she caught a whiff of her breath. "I need to brush my teeth."

Mrs. Andrews tilted her head to the bathroom. "Go ahead, dear. I'll have some food ready for you after you freshen up."

Cynthia walked to the bathroom. Other than her foul-smelling breath, she felt fine. She must have slept through any side effects of the egg harvesting.

The egg harvesting! How many eggs did she get? Were there any complications? Why didn't she remember yesterday? Had the doctor sent anything home with her? What embarrassing things did she say to Mark?

Cynthia leaned on the bathroom counter and caught her reflection in the mirror. Her hair stuck out in every direction. Dark circles rested under her eyes. Pimples dotted her cheeks, a reminder that her body was in hormonal overload.

"Basically, I resemble my life—a mess."

Tearing her eyes from the mirror, Cynthia brushed her teeth and made a mental list of questions she needed answered. Hopefully, the doctor had told Mark how everything went, and Mark had told his mother. As much as she appreciated his help, it seemed weird having to call him for news about her eggs. Especially when the memory of yesterday's hug popped into her head. She knew without a doubt that her crush on him was alive and well.

"How could you let that happen?" she asked herself after she put her toothbrush back in the cabinet.

She turned on the faucet and let the water get warm before she washed her face. As if she could scrub away her feelings as easily as yesterday's makeup. Not that she'd worn any to the doctor's office, but the point was now she needed to know what, if anything, she'd said during the car ride home.

Had she professed her undying love and devotion to him? She cringed at the thought. How embarrassing would it be to know that Mark knew the truth about her feelings, but she couldn't remember saying it?

She patted her face dry and smoothed on moisturizer. Surely, he would blame it on the anesthesia. No one could be held accountable for what they said under the influence of medication.

That was a good angle for the story. She grabbed her trusty pen and paper from the bathroom drawer and recorded the idea for later.

Stuffing the paper into her pocket, Cynthia headed back to the kitchen where she heard the sizzle of bacon and smelled the tantalizing scent of cinnamon.

"I hope you don't mind, but I've been following the aftercare procedures the doctor sent with you," said Mrs. Andrews. "You worried me when you got home, and Mark was no help at all. Sometimes I wonder about that boy." She turned away from the stove and pointed at a glass on the breakfast bar. "Here's some orange juice. The take-home information said you might be tired for a while; O. J. always peps me up."

Cynthia took a sip of the juice before asking, "Do you happen to know where my phone is?"

"Mark put it on the table by the front door. He wasn't sure where you normally kept it."

Her cheeks warmed at the sound of his name, but she refused to let herself ask where he was. Instead, she said, "Did he get any information from the doctor about how the procedure went?"

Mrs. Andrews slid the eggs and bacon out of the pan and onto a plate before setting it in front of her.

"He said the nurse didn't tell him much other than everything was fine and you needed rest." She handed Cynthia a packet. "This is what came home with you, and if you have any questions, they said to call."

Cynthia looked longingly at the food, but she had to know whether the day before had been a success. She sorted through the papers and leaflets until she came up with a document titled "Procedure Summary." A quick skim told her everything had, in fact, gone well, and the doctor had retrieved nine eggs.

"Good news, then?"

Mrs. Andrews's voice startled her.

"Yep. All went well. I need to call tomorrow for more details, but mission accomplished." She took another sip of juice before she said, "I should tell Mark thanks for driving me yesterday." She took a bite of the eggs as she waited for a response.

Mrs. Andrews opened the door to the stove and pulled out a pan of the biggest cinnamon rolls Cynthia ever seen.

"I'll let those cool before I put the frosting on. Plus, you don't want to burn your mouth." She wiped her hands on the apron she was wearing. "I'll be sure to pass on your thanks. Mark went home this morning."

Disappointment overrode the elation she'd been feeling.

To cover the frown she knew was on her face, Cynthia put a napkin to her mouth and dabbed her lips.

"Did you get to go antiquing at all?"

"Betty and I will go next weekend. From what I hear, Eveline cleaned out the good silver, anyway." Mrs. Andrews saved Cynthia from having to talk anymore as she listed all the reasons Eveline should no longer be allowed first access to any sales in town.

By the time Cynthia had finished her food, Mrs. Andrews plopped a steaming cinnamon roll onto her plate.

"Thank you for helping me, Mrs. Andrews. You didn't have to do all this."

"I know. But you deserve a break now and then. Pardon my nosiness," Mrs. Andrews said as she washed the dishes in the sink, "but why isn't your mother helping you?"

"Let's just say she isn't a proponent of what I'm doing."

"Threw the what-will-people-think card in your face, did she?"

Cynthia blew on the roll before shrugging. The guess was close enough.

"Don't let her get you down," said Mrs. Andrews. "Cybil made her own choices and had to live with the consequences. Make sure you make better choices. Now, I'm heading back to my place to let you get some more rest. I'll be there if you need me."

When Mrs. Andrews had left her alone with the warm pastry, Cynthia contemplated her comment. What did she mean? What choices had Cybil made? The only one Cynthia could think of was making her move out. But that decision was working out quite well for Cynthia—possibly too well, as she considered how many calories her breakfast contained.

She'd worry about that tomorrow. Right now, she was going to enjoy the day off from work and relax.

Chapter 23

The extra sleep on Sunday made the first part of Cynthia's week a breeze.

She patiently handled Thomas when he called first thing Monday morning. "I do appreciate your help, Thomas, but I've got a second date with Nick. It doesn't seem right to set up any new dates."

"What if it goes south? Wouldn't you like to have a backup plan?"

She tapped her pen on her notepad in aggravation. "That sounds like a rom-com. Look, I know you're bound by contract to help me, but I need to see this date through. There might be a trend out there, but dating more than one person doesn't work for everyone."

"True, but my knowledge of the business has shown me it's good to be prepared. Now, Nick has been with me a little over six months. He has a high second-date conversion, but third dates drop off dramatically. I'm looking out for you, Cynthia. That's all."

As much as she didn't want to admit it, Thomas did have more experience in this area.

"Fine. But let me get through the second date first. If

Thursday night goes south, you can set me up with someone else."

"Three someone elses. Your profile is knocking it out of the park."

She didn't remember setting up a profile, but if it was working, she decided to leave well enough alone.

On Tuesday, she acclimated to Jason and his new look. After his trip to the RuPaul show, he had begun to wear drag to work.

Several of the older customers complained to Dan about it, but he didn't seem to care.

"So long as Jason is getting his job done, more power to him." Cynthia had to agree when Dan added, "The man looks good in sequins."

The bonus of Jason's new outfits was that she could hear him coming. His high heels clicked on the floors, giving her plenty of notice when he was delivering news.

"Roger Gerome called. His name was spelled wrong in the weekly bowling scores. Said you should be more careful when you write up the column."

Cynthia shook her head. "Did you tell him I don't write that column, nor do I edit it? Phil should be getting these messages, not me."

"I did, but Roger insisted I tell you. For some reason, he thinks you run the show over here." Jason pushed up the sleeve of his fuchsia satin jacket and cocked his hip to one side. "Last week, Dan explained to Roger that you work for him, but Roger wanted nothing to do with it. He said as far as he was concerned, you were the only person he planned to contact."

"'Harass' is more like it." She took the message from Jason's hand, admiring his nail polish, and put it on her desk. "Nice color. I'll deal with this never."

Her meeting with Helene about the wedding dress database on Wednesday didn't bother her, either. While she would never use it, Cynthia knew many young brides would be thrilled to have a tool to help with the selection process.

"I'm telling you, there is a formula for dress selection. Too many people don't understand that if you don't get the right dress, the entire ceremony will feel it." Helene chatted on about how essential selecting the correct shade of white was. "It is an atrocity how many brides can't tell the difference between natural white, champagne, and alabaster."

Cynthia could think of other things she considered atrocities, but she let it go. Everyone needed something to care about, and shades of white were what Helene seemed to be focused on now.

"How did your egg harvesting go?"

The change in conversation surprised Cynthia, but she went with it.

"Good. I've got nine eggs on ice, figuratively speaking. Some great experiences for the article as well. I think this one will be a winner."

Helene leaned over and covered her hand. "This doesn't just have to be about winning. You could start a family now if you wanted."

Cynthia looked at their hands together. It dawned on her how foreign contact like this seemed. The Anderson family didn't touch. They didn't talk much either.

Letting out a sigh, Cynthia shook her head. "I could, but I've got a lot on my plate. This was always about the story. Besides, I wouldn't know what to do with a kid."

"That's not true and you know it." Helene squeezed her hand, then let it go. "But don't forget about Brad and Carlton. You could be Auntie Cyndi. Now, back to the dresses."

They moved on to a discussion of what technical development they needed when Cynthia remembered Grady, her date from the previous week, who was an IT consultant. She dug out his number for Helene and suggested she give him a call. She didn't know if this was exactly up his alley, but

Cynthia felt like he could point Helene in the right direction.

Cynthia agreed to take Helene's next meeting with Dr. Austen as well.

"Max is taking me to Chicago next week to see Sara. I feel bad asking Dr. Austen to reschedule, and you seemed to get along with her so well the last time. Do you mind?"

Cynthia added it to her calendar and chewed on her lip while Helene gathered her things.

"Do you think Brad and Carlton would really be interested in using one of my eggs?" she asked.

Helene looked at her with a smile. "Darling, you would be doing them a huge favor. Of course they would be interested. Give them a call and talk about it."

As if on cue, Cynthia's phone rang.

"It would be awesome if that were Brad, wouldn't it?" she called after Helene, who waved goodbye. Cynthia ran back to her desk and snatched up her phone. "Good morning. This is Cynthia Anderson. How can I help you?"

"For starters, you can stop by the house after work tomorrow." Her mother's voice grated in her ear. "And stop with that sing-song voice. It's annoying."

Cynthia flopped back in her chair. She didn't expect a preamble or an apology, but either would have been better than being ordered around and insulted.

"It's nice to talk to you, too, Mom. To what do I owe this pleasure?"

"Save it. I need you to go up in the attic and bring down some boxes for me. Then you can catch up my grade book. Ina May gave me until Friday. If it's not done by then, she's going to make me meet with the computer teacher, who smells like tuna, and he's going to teach me how to do it myself. You and I both know that's a bad idea."

"As much as I appreciate the invitation, I'm busy tomorrow night."

She pulled the phone away from her ear when her mother laughed.

"You're never busy. Don't even pretend to be mad about moving out of the house. Everyone around town tells me you're fine. Apparently, Mary Beth is feeding you so well, you've put on weight. Better be careful with that, young lady. Once you get to a certain age, the weight doesn't come off."

Leave it to her mother to call for a favor and end up berating her instead. Cynthia counted to five as she took a deep breath.

"My new place is lovely. Thanks for asking. I hear my old room is still empty, though. Something about a new location for your studio . . ."

"That's none of your business, but since someone bothered to gossip to you, your room is going to be my office. The studio works better at the wedding venue."

Not surprised that her mother would have a ready answer, Cynthia moved on. "I still can't come by tomorrow. I have a date, thanks to you renewing the contract with Thomas. He's upped his game, and I've been on four dates in the last week."

The line fell silent. At first, she thought they'd been disconnected, but she could hear her mother breathing.

"What? You don't want to gloat?"

"Thomas really is batty."

"Mom, he hasn't done anything wrong."

"He lied to you."

"No, I'd say he's the only person who *hasn't* lied to me lately."

Cybil's voice went up a pitch. "He did—because I didn't renew your contract."

Cynthia paused. She didn't know anyone else who would shell out $5,000, which was the going rate the last time she'd asked Thomas about it. Even if he was running the same promotion he'd had when Cybil and Helene went in on it together, no one's name popped into her head.

Deciding that was a mystery for another day, she returned to her mother's request.

"Well, I have a date tomorrow night. Best I can do is come by on Friday, which doesn't sound like it's going to help you. Maybe learning how to do it yourself is a good thing."

The sound of fingernails drumming on the counter echoed across the line. If she were sitting in front of her mother right now, the noise would irritate her and make her break down and agree. But over the phone, Cynthia didn't feel the pressure. She sat and waited for her mother to make the next move.

Dan popped his head in the door. "Need you in the conference room. Emergency meeting. Phil can't handle Roger. You're getting the sports column for the rest of the year."

"Roger?" squawked Cybil. "He's there?"

Cynthia breathed a sigh of relief at the interruption. "Sorry, Mom. Gotta go."

"Do not hang up on—"

She dropped the phone into the cradle and stood up. "You lead the way." She gestured to Dan as she picked up her notepad and paper. "Best not let Phil stew for too long."

Dan followed her out. "You sure that was a good idea? Your mother doesn't like being told what to do."

Cynthia shrugged. "It'll be fine. What's the worst that could happen?"

Chapter 24

Turns out the worst that could happen was a scream fest with Phil. The harassed sports reporter refused to cover bowling anymore, and it took both Dan and Cynthia the rest of the afternoon to calm him.

"Cynthia needs to deal with that tyrant! He asks for her all the time. Give him what he wants and make everyone's lives easier."

"That would make *your* life easier and *mine* more difficult," she countered. "Plus, my plate is already full. I have my usual assignments, plus helping Helene with her wedding column, and I've got the egg-harvesting piece. Where am I supposed to fit in the sports column?"

"You don't get the sports column. You only get Roger," Phil spat at her before he turned to Dan. "Tell her she has to do it. Or I'm leaving."

Cynthia's eyes whipped to Dan's face to gauge his reaction. She relaxed when he winked at her.

"You're not going anywhere, Phil. I'll admit Roger is being a pain in the keister right now, but that's part of your job. Convince him you can handle it. Apologize for the misspellings. Have Jason proofread your stuff before you send it to the proofreader."

"I never use a proofreader."

That comment wrapped up their meeting. Cynthia acquiesced to Phil's request that she call Roger and explain why she couldn't be his point of contact.

By the time she made it back to her desk to contact Roger, she had four voicemail messages from her mother. She was surprised to hear the progression of the messages.

"I cannot believe you hung up on me. Call me back this instant." There was a long pause before Cybil added, *"This is your mother,"* then she slammed down the phone.

"As if I wouldn't know," Cynthia mumbled as she deleted the message and moved to the next.

"What is the matter with you lately? Didn't I teach you to be respectful?"

"No, you did not," Cynthia said, and listened to the next message. She wasn't surprised to hear her mother had changed tactics.

"I could lose my job if you don't help me. Do you really want to be responsible for that? Really, helping me is the least you could do. I kept a roof over your head for far longer than I needed to."

"And kicked me out with little notice."

Cynthia rested her head on her desk. Guilt used to work. It might still work, but there was no way she was giving up a second date to deal with her mother's problem. This could have been prevented years ago, but Cybil had refused to listen.

The last message caught Cynthia's attention.

"You won't understand this because you don't have children, but everything I've done for you, even having you move out of the house, I did for your own good. You don't have to like it, but it's the truth." She heard her mother take a deep breath before she asked, *"Now, can you please come over tomorrow?"*

"Don't do it."

Dan's voice caused her to whip her head up so fast she felt a twinge in her neck.

"You'll regret it if you do," he added.

Without bothering to answer, she sighed. "I haven't called Roger yet. I need to gather my strength first."

"He can wait a few minutes." Dan settled himself into her chair and shook his head. "Does she always sound so pathetic? Sorry if that comes across as rude, but man, I thought *my* mother was bad."

Cynthia tucked that tidbit of information away for a rainy day.

"She doesn't always sound like that, but Cybil Anderson is a master at the art of manipulation." Her eyebrows raised as she stared at her editor. "Sort of like you making me call Roger."

He waved aside the remark. "I'll call him. I planned to the entire time, but I didn't want Phil to know. He whines almost as much as Roger does." He crossed his leg over his knee and steepled his fingers in front of him. "I gave you a couple days, but I wanted to check in. How did the doctor appointment go?"

She should have known he wouldn't forget. There was a lot riding on this story.

"Fine. The procedure extracted nine eggs, and I'm considering a donation to a couple in need. If they're willing, I'll follow them on their journey as well. Good angle for the story, and it takes me out of the spotlight."

"Only considering? I figured Helene got a promise in blood you'd carry a child for Brad and Carlton."

Her eyes felt cartoonishly large, like they were going to pop out of her head.

"That woman has no filter, does she? And it's an egg. I'm not signing up to be a surrogate."

Dan pointed at her. "You would've gone along with it if I hadn't shut it down."

Keeping up with all the ins and outs of Helene's antics was pointless, so she shrugged. "I'm waiting on my genetics test to come back first. If all is well, I'll make the offer."

Dan nodded. "Good call. Who wants defective eggs?"

Rolling her eyes, Cynthia asked, "Anything else I can do, or can I go home for the day?"

"Go home." He stood up. "And since I'm feeling generous, why don't you work from home tomorrow? I need your revisions for Helene's columns, and you need to first-draft your procedure experience. If I know Phil and Roger, tomorrow will be another fun-filled day of whining and complaining."

She relished the thought of a quiet day at home. Spending Sunday in bed had given her too much insight into what life without responsibilities would be. Too bad she could only visit that world and not live in it.

Chapter 25

Cynthia touched up her lip gloss. She couldn't believe how smoothly her day had gone. Working from home made everything go faster. Not only had she gotten all her work completed, as well as some additional research into the legal issues facing surrogacy, she'd also had time for a nap and shower before she got ready for her date with Nick and still arrived at the steakhouse early.

The lighting in the restaurant's bathroom left a lot to be desired, but she smoothed down her hair and gave herself a nod before she checked in.

The hostess, her natural red hair artfully arranged in a way Cynthia could never achieve, returned at the same time Nick appeared.

"Perfect timing." He leaned in and gave Cynthia a kiss on the cheek before saying, "Hi. We have a reservation."

The redhead turned the full force of her attention on Nick, ignoring Cynthia. It didn't really bother her, but it made her wonder why Nick would go along with it. He didn't seem to notice that the other woman was flirting with him. Even when they reached the table, the woman pulled out Nick's chair and let Cynthia fend for herself.

After they were seated and had ordered drinks, Nick smiled at her. "It's good to see you again. How was your day?"

"Productive. I worked from home and—"

Nick interrupted, frowning as if he had just learned she was an ex-convict. "I thought you worked at the newspaper. Don't you have an office?"

She nodded. "I do. But I had a bunch of writing and research to get through, so my editor told me to work at home. It's quieter."

She thought Nick seemed less enthusiastic in their conversation after that. He told her about the construction on the wedding venue and how stressful it was working with a bunch of opinionated ladies.

"They are the client though, right?" she couldn't help asking.

He shrugged. "I guess. But none of them seem to be able to make a decision. This is construction. We have to get things planned so we can order the right supplies. I don't have time to deal with a bunch of last-minute changes and additions."

Cynthia's cell phone rang, and she dug through her purse to find it. "Whoops. Meant to put that on silent."

Nick looked around the room and said in a loud voice, "That's rude. People are staring."

She glanced up as her hand found her phone. No one was looking in their direction except the hostess, who was flipping her curls over her shoulder and sending goo-goo eyes at Nick.

Dating was about learning, and Cynthia learned she must have missed a few things on their first date.

Cynthia glanced at the caller ID. *MOM.* Instead of answering, she turned the phone on silent and put it on the seat beside her. If she knew anything, her mother was not a quitter.

"Sorry. Won't happen again."

Their dinner arrived, and they ate and talked about their week. Nick did most of the talking and the eating, she noticed.

As he shared his day, which in her opinion sounded incredibly boring, he gobbled his food. In fact, his prime rib was gone before she'd taken a second bite of her filet. She started to ask him what the hurry was, but her phone vibrated. At least she could still predict her mother.

"What's that noise?" Nick asked. A partially masticated piece of meat hung out of the side of his mouth, and Cynthia quickly looked down at her plate.

Definitely no third date. How had she missed this hostile behavior last week?

"I don't hear anything," she said, and took another bite of her steak. "Hmm, dis is gud."

"You shouldn't talk with your mouth full," Nick said, and stood up. "I'm going to the john."

"That's nice," she mumbled, then glanced at caller ID.

Her mother. Again.

Looking up, she noticed Nick chatting with the hostess. That explained his sudden need to use the restroom. She sighed and muted her phone for a second time.

By the time Nick sauntered back to the table, she had five missed calls from her mother, and her steak was cold. It wasn't unusual for her mother to hound her like this, but she was starting to wonder what could be so important on a Thursday night that she kept calling.

She wasn't surprised when Nick slid into the seat across from her and announced, "I can't date someone who gets calls all during dinner. It's rude. You need to work on your social skills."

"Well, I was going to suggest that you might not want to get another woman's phone number while you're on a date. It's bad form."

Her phone rang again, and she decided she had nothing to lose. The date was over, so she might as well find out what was so urgent with her mother.

Cynthia answered the phone. "What do you want, Mom?"

"I told her to stop calling you."

She recognized Brad's voice, then looked at the caller ID. Instead of her mother's number, Brad's appeared.

"Sorry to bother you," he said, "but you need to go to the hospital. There's been an incident with your mom."

Cynthia stood up, her napkin falling to the floor.

"What kind of incident?"

"Who is that?" asked Nick. "Don't they know it's rude to interrupt dinner?"

"Who is that? Are you on a date?" asked Brad.

"His name is Nick, and the date is over. What happened?"

"Then I'm not paying for it. We could still turn this around," said Nick with a leer, "if you know what I mean."

"Yuck," said Brad. "I'll pay for dinner if you promise to leave right this minute. Where did you find that one?"

"Don't ask. I'm leaving now."

She hung up and stepped right into Nick, who was standing in front of her with his arms crossed.

"So what? You have a friend make a phone call if things go south on the date?"

"If only I had thought of that," Cynthia said as she pulled her credit card from her wallet and waved down the server. "No, my mother is at the hospital. I have to go see what's wrong, although she probably is faking an injury because she wanted me to blow off our date tonight so I could help her with her grade book."

Her cheeks warmed. Nick would never believe this was a coincidence now. Not that she cared.

He surprised her when he said, "I'll follow you over. I want to see exactly what is going on."

"Not necessary." She nodded to the hostess, who was anxiously watching the exchange between the two of them. "Besides, you have someone waiting for you."

"She doesn't get off until ten. I can bust you for lying and still get back here in time."

The server brought Cynthia's credit card back, and she signed the receipt.

"When you see I'm not lying, you can pay me for that prime rib you swallowed whole."

He waved her off. "Not gonna happen. This was a setup if I ever saw one. We're gonna get to the hospital and your mother won't be there."

Cynthia led the way out of the restaurant. As much as she wanted Nick to be right, something told her the night was about to get more complicated.

Chapter 26

Cynthia didn't bother to wait for Nick when she arrived at the hospital. She dashed straight to the emergency room and discovered her mother had already been admitted. The receptionist gave her the room number but had no details on Cybil's condition.

Nick sauntered up while she was waiting for the elevator. "All for nothing, I assume," he said when he stopped next to her.

"She's in room 324," Cynthia murmured. "You owe me for dinner."

"How am I going to know this is really your mother? I still think you set this up."

Cynthia tapped her foot as she waited for the elevator to arrive. "You've met Cybil Anderson, right? You'll recognize her." The doors opened, and she walked in. Nick just stood there, and she asked, "Are you coming or not?"

"I don't like elevators."

She pressed the button to hold open the door. "Don't care. Get in."

He pointed to the stairs. "I'll meet you. What floor?"

Cynthia threw up her free hand. "You have no intention of going to my mother's room, do you?"

Nick had the decency to stare at the floor when he said, "I thought you were lying to get out of the date or to get a free meal. No one's mother really ends up in the hospital. It's a story people tell to get out of something."

The elevator alarm went off, signaling the doors had been open for too long, and Cynthia let go of the button and stepped off the elevator.

"Fine. Pay me for your steak and leave. I can handle the rest myself."

Without argument, Nick pulled out several bills and slapped them into her hand before he turned and walked back down the hall.

She glanced at the money and cursed. He'd shorted her $10.

Cynthia turned back to the elevator and stabbed the *Call* button. Maybe this was a sign—a sign to never date again.

She made it to the third floor and heard her mother complaining as soon as she stepped out of the elevator.

"It's too cold in here. I need another blanket."

Cynthia prepared herself for her mother's bad mood and headed to the room. She made it to the door as a nurse walked out.

"This patient isn't ready for visitors," he told Cynthia.

"I'm her daughter."

The nurse's eyebrows raised as he appraised her. "So, you're the one she's been asking about for the last two hours?" He tilted his head toward the door. "Go ahead, and Godspeed. I'll be back to see how the pain is."

Cynthia didn't know if he was referring to her impending pain or her mother's existing pain, but the fact that Cybil had been here for two hours motivated her enough to walk through the door.

"Took you long enough to get here." Cybil pushed a button connected to her IV.

Cynthia watched as whatever was in the IV took effect. Her mother's face relaxed, the crow's feet around her eyes smoothing out and the lines across her forehead relaxing. Her mother's next words were calmer and slightly slurred.

"Cynthia, honey, come over here. I want to give you a hug."

Cynthia dropped her purse and jacket on the recliner at the end of the bed and walked to her mother's side. She leaned over to put her arms around her mother, but Cybil's hand flew out and slapped her.

"What the hell, Mom! That hurt!" She rubbed her arm. "I thought drugs were supposed to help with the pain, not inflict more of it."

Her mother reached forward, but Cynthia stepped back.

Cybil groaned and fell back against the pillows. "None of this would have happened if you behaved like a normal daughter. But no, I have to do everything myself."

Cynthia pushed her belongings off the chair and sat down. "Did you go up in the attic by yourself? I told you I would help tomorrow night. Why didn't you wait? And what happened anyway?"

Before Cybil could respond, a group of people paraded into the room.

"Ms. Anderson, I'm Dr. Barr. We spoke earlier. I assume this is your daughter," said the tallest man in the group.

Cynthia nodded. She'd never met him, but she'd heard his name around town. He was an excellent doctor, but from what Roger said, he sucked at golf and bowling.

"The X-rays confirmed a fractured right hip," Dr. Barr announced.

Cynthia gasped. "How did you do that?" she asked her mother.

"Fell down the attic stairs, thanks to you."

"I wasn't even there! How is it my fault?"

"Exactly."

Dr. Barr cleared his throat. "Anyway, this case seems straightforward. You'll need surgery. I've got an opening in a day, so hang tight and we'll get you all fixed up."

Before Cynthia could ask any questions, the door flew open again, and Betty and Helene burst into the room. Betty went straight to Cybil's side while Helene took hold of Dr. Barr's arm.

"Oh, I'm so glad you're here, Walter," she gushed. "We got here as soon as we heard. When are you taking her in for surgery? Please tell me you'll be in charge. I would *not* want to have that young whippersnapper in charge. Do you know what he did to Claude? After he replaced his hip, Claude couldn't bowl for the rest of the season. It made the Glen Geezers miss out on the championship round."

The doctor's face relaxed, and an easy smile brightened his previously serious demeanor.

"Good to see you, Helene. I'd never speak ill of my coworkers, but thanks for the support." He nodded toward Cybil. "You can get the details from Ms. Anderson. I'm heading out to the bowling league dinner tonight. Max is saving me a seat."

Dr. Barr and his entourage waltzed out of the room, and Helene rounded on Cybil.

"How on earth did you manage this, Cybil?"

Cybil shrugged and pointed at Cynthia. "Ask her. She thought a date was more important than helping her mother."

"Knock it off," said Betty. "I told you to wait for help, and you traipsed up to the attic anyway. Besides, you and I both know that pain pump has you on cloud nine right now." Betty winked at Cynthia when Cybil shrugged. "You should be nicer to your only child. She didn't have to come to the hospital, but she's here now."

Cybil squinted at Cynthia. "Where's your date? I thought you had a date tonight. Are you avoiding me?"

"Of course she's avoiding you," said Helene, "but I did see her date downstairs. He made sure she got to the hospital safely but didn't think it was right to come to your room. Very polite if you ask me."

Cynthia glanced at Helene.

Helene turned so Cybil couldn't see, and she put a finger to her lips, signaling Cynthia to be quiet.

Cynthia hoped there wasn't confusion on her face when she turned back to her mother.

"Helene's right. Nick went home as soon as I found out what room you were in."

For a second, Cynthia worried her mother would ask more questions about her date, but Cybil had moved on.

She was peering into Betty's bag. "Did you bring me a scone or a muffin? I missed dinner, and the ambulance wouldn't stop at a drive-through."

"Mom, you can't eat before surgery!" said Cynthia. "You know that."

Her mother shook her head. "According to Dr. Barr, I'm not having surgery until tomorrow." She pointed at the clock. "Could be hours before they're ready for me."

Betty shook her head. "Your daughter's right. Nothing for you." She held out a white bakery sack to Cynthia. "But that doesn't stop me from sharing with everyone else. We could all do with some comfort food about now."

Cynthia took Betty's offering, and, for the first time, the situation felt real to her. Her mother was lying in bed with a broken hip. Her mother's friends were more in control than she was.

She peeked into the bag. A chocolate-almond croissant stared back at her. Moving to the corner of the room, as far from her mother as possible, she turned her back and ripped off a chunk of the pastry. Stuffing it into her mouth, she closed her eyes and enjoyed the taste. It might be the last one she had for a while. Or it might be one of many she used to soothe herself when the going got tough. Only time would tell.

Chapter 27

"Thank you for helping me with those medical forms," said Cynthia as she munched a second chocolate croissant. She'd regret all the stress-eating later, but it was making her feel good right now. "I'm not sure how I was supposed to finish them with a time limit hanging over my head."

"Try saving your marriage while you're on the clock," Helene said as she picked at a scone. "These really are tremendous, Betty. I don't know how you pack so much flavor into them. Oh wait, I do remember—copious amounts of butter and a jillion calories. My rear says I hate you, but my heart is loving this."

Betty sat back in the recliner. The women had the hospital room to themselves while Cybil was down in CT. Even though surgery would take place the next morning, Dr. Barr wanted some scans taken, so he knew exactly what he was facing.

"Those scones make me a ton of money but have cost me a few patrons. Eveline refuses to come back to the Coffee Bar because, word on the street is, her yoga pants went up a size."

Cynthia shook her head. "Why is she still wearing yoga pants? She's the one who said women over fifty shouldn't wear tight clothes. What's tighter than yoga pants? Other than my jeans with each bite of this croissant?"

"My, you sound as bitter as Sara before she got married," Helene said. "Maybe you should step away from the pastry for a bit and find a group of younger women to spend time with. If you keep hanging around us, you may miss your forties and fifties altogether."

Betty laughed. "Now, Helene, I'm not that much older than you, and I'm not a day over twenty-nine."

Cynthia ignored the women as they joked about their ages. Truth be told, she did need some friends her own age, but she planned to put that on the to-do list after she'd won her third journalism award.

The door opened, and Cybil was rolled in on a bed by two twenty-something male orderlies.

"Cynthia, you need to meet Roberto and Eric." Cybil gestured at the men.

Roberto gave her a brief nod before he locked the hospital bed into place. Eric, on the other hand, walked straight to Cynthia and took her hand. She liked the way her skin tingled when Eric squeezed her hand.

"Your mother is proud of you. We heard all about the relationship coordinator you work with."

Helene and Betty burst out laughing.

"Why would you tell a perfectly good candidate that you signed your daughter up with Thomas?" Helene asked Cybil. "Did I not provide a bad enough example for you with Sara?"

Cybil waved off the comment. "I keep telling you, I didn't sign her up this time. But she needs options. I didn't have options when I was her age."

Betty shook her head. "No, but that was your choice. You were a single mother by then. Cynthia doesn't seem to be following in your footsteps."

Cynthia felt her cheeks flame up in embarrassment at the realization her mother's friends were talking about her lack of sex life in front of a well-built, attractive man who probably had sex on a regular basis.

Eric dropped her hand and gave her a salute. "I work second shift. Depending on how long your mother is here, I might see you again." He followed a silent Roberto out the door.

"Well, are you going to jump on that?" asked Betty. "Because if you don't, I might. He is *cute*."

Cynthia cringed at the thought of Betty and Eric together. Betty was the best pastry chef in the county and a wonderful woman, but the thought of her having sex made Cynthia push aside the croissant she was eating.

Sort of like thinking about her mother with a man. Completely appetite-killing.

She stood up and threw the rest of the pastry in the trash.

"Any word on when surgery will be?" she asked her mother.

"Dr. Barr saw me in the hallway. Someone is reading the scan thingy and will let me know tonight."

Cybil reached for a muffin, but Betty pulled the basket away.

"What? I'm hungry," she complained. "We don't know when surgery will be. This is cruel and unusual punishment, even for you."

"Complain all you will," said Betty, "but you need to be ready when the doctors are." She pulled a deck of cards out of her purse. "What if we distract you with poker? Maybe I can win some money off you while you're loopy."

Cybil pushed herself up and groaned. "I might be drugged up, but you won't be taking my money. Everyone knows you have no poker face."

Cynthia slipped out of the hospital room before the women could rope her into playing cards, thankful that someone could keep her mother company.

Cynthia needed to use the time to let Dan know what was

happening. The pamphlet the nurse had given her said to expect twenty-four to forty-eight hours in the hospital post-hip-replacement and then a few weeks of home recovery. Despite their differences, Cynthia knew she would be on night duty while her mother recuperated. Might as well let Dan know now. She didn't want to give him any excuse to complain later.

Hoping to find a quiet bench outside where her phone would get better reception, Cynthia made her way to the elevator. She texted Dan, then scrolled through her emails while she waited. Nothing important popped up.

There was a follow-up reminder to call Carl Raeburn. She'd written a story on his Women's Shelter and Support Agency. Even though the agency was in Las Vegas, Cynthia had pitched the story because Sara Shaw, Helene's daughter, was involved. Dan fell for the hometown angle every single time.

Cynthia also hoped they could set up something in Glen Valley for women in need. A small town kept out some of the chaos of big city life, but there were still women whose husbands weren't supportive or were downright abusive. Mr. Raeburn's model for operating low-cost housing for single mothers seemed like something even Glen Valley could use.

Even though Cynthia was busy with the egg-harvesting story, she felt like she should spare the time for the women's shelter too.

The ping of elevator doors opening made Cynthia step forward, but instead of finding herself in the elevator car, she bumped into something tall and firm.

Looking up, she smiled. "Sorry, Brad, I wasn't paying attention to where I was going."

Chapter 28

Brad took her arm and looked down at her. "Didn't mean to run into you like that." His arms dropped to his sides. "How's your mom?"

She felt her face crinkle in dismay. "I should have called you with an update. She broke her hip and is scheduled for surgery in the morning," She blinked several times before she asked, "What are you doing here, anyway?"

He pushed back his hair with one hand, and Cynthia noticed his pale face.

"When I hadn't heard from you, Carlton told me I should just come up here," he said. "I feel terrible for what happened."

To lighten the mood, she cocked her hip and pointed her finger accusingly at him. "Are you telling me you pushed her down the attic stairs? As far as I can see, that's the only way you could have been involved."

"That's not exactly what happened."

A man pushed past them into the elevator, and Cynthia put out her arm to keep the doors from closing.

"I'm heading downstairs. Want to join me?"

Brad nodded and got back on the elevator.

"She's stable," Cynthia continued. "They're doing some tests before the procedure." She gestured upward. "Helene and Betty are playing poker with her if you want to join them. I trust you don't need the warning that they are card sharks, and your money is fair game."

He laughed. "No way I'm getting into a card game with Helene. Carlton and I played her and Max last weekend, and it was a disaster. They cleaned us out."

They rode the rest of the way down in silence, stopping once to let people on and off. By the time they got to the lobby, Cynthia had responded to several texts and emails on her phone.

"You're popular tonight," he said as he led the way out of the elevator. "Everything okay?"

She nodded and paused outside the gift shop, right in front of the hand-blown vases displayed in the window.

"Yeah. I let Dan know what's happening with my mother so we can shuffle things around. He had a question about Helene's next column. She has a couple things to revise, but I told him I'd do it since she's keeping my mom busy."

Cynthia shifted. It was hard to admit she was more at ease away from her mother than with her.

"That was nice of you," Brad agreed, "but maybe you should spend some time with her. She misses having you around." When her eyes flew to his face, he shrugged. "What? That's what she told me."

Cynthia wanted to ask if he was telling the truth, but instead she turned and headed to the exit.

"Come on. Let's get out of here."

She led him to the ramada, the structure Brad had built the previous year. In the dark, the reflection pool twinkled with landscape lighting. The yellows, pinks, and purples of the plants and shrubs were dim, but they reminded anyone who looked at them of the warmer summer weather. The colors were still a contrast to the simple shade structure Brad had designed using native rock and stone. The reclaimed wood from an old hospital fence stood proudly as the focal point for the only wall of the structure.

"I don't know how you did it, but this is the most relaxing spot in the place," said Cynthia as she walked to the park bench. Her eyes closed and her face smoothed as she relaxed into the seat. "And you picked good furniture. So much better than the stupid visitor chairs upstairs."

She waited until he sat down next to her. Cynthia needed to know why he was really here.

Before she could ask, he blurted out, "Cynthia, I want you to know I'm sorry. I didn't mean for your mother to get hurt."

Her left eye opened, and she drawled, "You still haven't explained what you have to be sorry about." She didn't have to wait long to find out what was bothering him.

"She asked me to help her with something from the attic. I told her I didn't have time. She went up on her own and fell down the stairs. When you didn't answer, she called me, and I called 911. I feel horrible. It's my fault."

Cynthia snorted loudly enough that Brad jumped.

"It's *her* fault," she corrected him. "Don't let her make you feel guilty. I told her I would help her on Saturday, but she wouldn't wait."

"She told me you said you were busy Saturday."

"And you believe everything you hear? Besides, she's the one that fell. She should have called 911 herself." Cynthia shuddered and closed her eyes. "Doing it this way gets her more attention."

He cleared his throat. "For what it's worth, I don't agree with turning your room into the office for the pottery studio."

Both of Cynthia's eyes popped open this time. "Really? And how did my mother take that bit of news?"

He squirmed in his chair. "She sounded a bit accusatory, like you did just now."

Cynthia chuckled and rolled her eyes. "Fine. There might

be something to that. I know you're the only architect in town, but I still feel a little betrayed. Thank you for trying to save my room."

"Well, I didn't exactly save it. I told your mother that converting the room would lower the house value, not to mention cost her money she doesn't need to spend. The wedding venue has enough space for what she needs. I didn't go over to her house tonight because I thought she was still trying to convince me we could make it work."

Sitting up, Cynthia sighed. "What is it about parents? They never listen, do they?"

A companionable silence fell between the two of them, intersected by the noises of the night. A frog croaked, crickets chirped, and an ambulance wailed. Cynthia glanced over at Brad, but he seemed lost in his own thoughts. Maybe he was thinking about his own parents and the things they never paid attention to.

She'd almost forgotten where they left the conversation when Brad said quietly, "No, they don't listen. What did Cybil not listen to you about?"

Shaking her head, Cynthia said, "The list is endless. But it doesn't matter. For now, it looks like I'll be taking care of her for a few days after surgery. Now, enough about me. How's it going with you and Carlton and making babies?"

He chuckled at her change in topic. "Well, Dr. Purdue is great. He suggested we get a separate egg donor and surrogate. Our last attempt was to get them together, but he thought we'd have better luck this way."

"Why's that?"

"It's less likely the surrogate changes her mind. That's what happened last time. We made it through the entire evaluation process and were going to meet her in Chicago when she called it off. She decided she couldn't give up her own child."

"I'm surprised that wasn't vetted earlier in the process," Cynthia said.

"It was, but surrogates can still change their minds. It happens. We think she realized the baby was for two men and that's why she flaked, but we don't have any proof." He shrugged. "Anyway, Carlton and I are going through the egg donor files now. It's exciting, but there is a long waiting list. You're lucky—you'll have your own eggs, so when you're ready to start a family, you won't have to wait."

She tapped him on the shoulder. "Maybe you could use one of my eggs, so you don't have to wait either."

Chapter 29

The stunned expression on Brad's face told Cynthia she'd done the right thing.

"Are you serious? A donated egg from a healthy woman is *huge*."

Cynthia held up her hand. "The downside is that I know nothing about my father's side of the family. I'm waiting on genetic testing, but my dad could be an ogre for all I know."

"I don't think that's the case, but I appreciate the warning. If you're serious, I'll talk to Carlton." He hesitated. "You know that most women are compensated for donating their eggs, right?"

She hoped her next comment wouldn't put him off, but she needed his and Carlton's agreement for the complete story.

"I have a better idea. I'm already planning a series—Helene actually recommended it: A first-person perspective of egg retrieval. The cost of fertility. The struggle of a same-sex couple trying to have a baby. It would be a strong contender for next year's investigative reporting awards."

When Brad didn't answer, she got nervous.

"I'm sorry. I got a little carried away. You can still have an egg even if you don't want me to do the story."

A smile passed over his face, and he shook his head. "It's not that. I'd be happy to be part of the story. We'd have to talk to Carlton, but I think he'd be willing as well. It doesn't seem like enough, though." He paused as if he were considering something. "Do you need a . . . donor?"

It took her a minute to figure out what Brad was referring to, and her face warmed when it clicked.

"No. This is for the story. I'm not mother material."

"That's crap and you know it. So, when you change your mind, I'm happy to help. It's the least I can do."

"You're welcome. Talk to Carlton—make sure everything is okay with him—and let me know. My eggs aren't going anywhere, but I'm going to put a call into the doctor and let him know the plan. If you call him, too, and leave him a, uh, *sample*, he can run whatever tests are needed to make sure they can . . . ," she hesitated, not sure how to complete her thought, "play nicely together."

Brad nodded and relaxed back onto the bench. "I'll do that.

"You know, Cybil will need your help during her recovery," he added. "It doesn't sound like she has the resources for a lot of outside medical help."

Cynthia knew her mother had saved for a rainy day, but she didn't have a clue how much. Cybil didn't take risks with her money, but she would need everything she had for the business venture, which meant she wouldn't want to spend money on herself.

"I don't know," Cynthia replied. "This incident is going to cost her a chunk of change, but she won't want to go to an assisted living facility or rehab, even for a little bit. Cybil Anderson won't ask for help, even for something like this."

Brad shook his head. "She's not going to get the option. The doctor won't release her until she's ready, and the insurance company will want her out of the hospital before then.

The only other choice is for her to go home, but she has to have someone there to help her."

Cynthia slumped back on the bench. As much as she hated to admit it, Brad was right: her mother needed her. There wasn't anyone else. Cynthia's grandparents were long gone, and she had no aunts or uncles. Cybil's friend group was supportive—Helene and Betty could be counted on to help, as could a few people from Bunco and school—but the bulk of the responsibility would be on Cynthia, whether she liked it or not.

"You're right. And she actually spoke to me when I was in the hospital room. That's progress, right?"

They sat for a few more minutes before Brad's phone rang. He looked down and said, "I've got to take this. Carlton and I will talk about your offer and get back to you. Thank you so much." He gave her a quick hug before walking away to take the call.

Cynthia leaned back and tilted her head to the sky. It wasn't often she sat outside in the evening to watch the stars twinkle and to enjoy the calm of nature. Granted, she was sitting outside of a hospital, so that wasn't the most serene of settings, but she did feel like she understood what was happening for the first time in a while.

She was needed. By her mother. Something she'd given up on happening. She might be getting ahead of herself, since she hadn't talked to Cybil about this, but Brad was right that she was the logical person to do it.

Cynthia couldn't help but think her mother would be pleased that she'd offered to give an egg to Brad and Carlton. Cybil was always telling her to be more generous. If this gesture wasn't altruistic, Cynthia didn't know what was.

With a spring in her step, she headed back to her mother's room. She wouldn't share anything about her plan until after the surgery, but this was something she and her mother couldn't argue about—she hoped.

Chapter 30

The next morning, Cynthia drove back to the hospital for her mother's hip surgery. They had agreed to a truce, and Cybil had sent her home to pack a bag for a few days.

Mrs. Andrews had caught Cynthia as she was leaving the house and handed her a cooler full of homemade goodies, so she wouldn't have to go to the cafeteria. She was skeptical but pleased that Cynthia had decided to stay with her mother while she recovered.

"Your mother is a hard one to deal with, but I'm glad you're taking the high road."

Mrs. Andrews's words came to fruition the moment Cynthia stepped into Cybil's hospital room.

"You seem awfully chipper this morning. Don't get too used to being home. I'll be back soon, and you can go back to that apartment of yours," Cybil said as she picked at the IV in her arm. "This thing hurts. You'd think after all this time someone would figure out how to make one that didn't."

Cynthia ignored the complaint. Her mother's usual grouchiness was enhanced by pain and nervousness about the surgery. She couldn't help complaining.

Although she complained even when she didn't have a broken hip.

Rather than dwell on it, Cynthia did what Mrs. Andrews had suggested. She leaned in and gave her mother a kiss.

Cybil froze. "What was that for?"

She shrugged. "For luck. Am I not allowed to do that?"

Cybil crossed her arms over her chest. The movement pulled on the IV, and she winced in pain. "Damn it. That hurt." She looked at Cynthia. "I think you're saying goodbye."

Knowing it would start a fight, but also knowing it was true, Cynthia nodded. "Fine. Yes. I want to make sure I say goodbye in case something happens. I'd prefer we were on good terms before Dr. Barr takes you down to OR, but if you want to be stubborn about it, fine—how about I flip you off as you leave the room?"

Cybil rewarded her with a deep belly laugh. "I wondered how long it would take you to get back to normal. All this sympathy is giving me a stomachache."

Glad they were on familiar ground, Cynthia said, "Your stomach hurts because you haven't eaten in forty-eight hours."

Cybil nodded at the IV in her other arm. "They say I'm getting plenty of calories from whatever is in that thing, but if I can't taste it, it doesn't count."

There was a knock on the door, and Eric, the orderly, popped his head in. "Hi. Didn't know if I would see you today."

Roberto entered the room and made a beeline for Cybil while Eric continued to speak to Cynthia.

"We need to get her to surgery," he explained. "You can wait here if you want or in the family room."

"She's going to stay here to save my spot," piped up Cybil, who glared at Roberto when he raised the side rail on her bed. "Watch out. That thing pinches."

Eric shot Cynthia a smile, then turned to Cybil. "Let's get

you to the OR. They have some very good drugs that will make you feel like a million bucks."

As the two men pushed Cybil out of the room, she called back, "Remember, Cynthia—don't let anyone take my room!"

"Okay. Will do," Cynthia said, and rolled her eyes.

There was no telling what her mother would say in the operating room. She hoped it had nothing to do with her.

She settled down in the side chair and started on her work. She managed to edit all of Helene's columns before someone knocked on the door. A quick glance at the clock told her it was too soon for news of her mother.

"Come in," she called.

Eric entered the room, and she frowned.

"Is everything okay with my mom?" she asked.

He nodded. "As far as I know. Roberto and I dropped her in pre-op, and I heard her tell the charge nurse that the floor wasn't clean enough. Sally told her it was a good thing they weren't operating on the floor."

Cynthia laughed. "That sounds like my mom." She glanced around the room. "Do you need something?"

He shifted from one foot to another. He seemed nervous. "Actually, I'm on break." He held out a pager. "I snagged you one of these from the family waiting room. The nurse there will page you when your mom's surgery is finished and when you should head to post-op. I thought if you had one of these you might be able to join me for coffee in the cafeteria."

She blinked. It sounded like Eric was asking her on a date. To the hospital cafeteria. During her mother's surgery.

She blinked again when she considered how unusual her surge of recent dates had been and then nodded. Might as well embrace the strange.

"Sure," she said. Standing up, she took the pager and slipped it into her bag with her laptop and notes. Most of her work was finished. Why not have a cup of coffee with the hot orderly who seemed capable of handling her mother's snarky and rude behavior? "You lead the way."

Eric smiled, and, for the first time, Cynthia realized how nervous he was.

The expression on his face relaxed, and his posture straightened. He held the door open for her and walked beside her down the hall to the elevator.

"If you want, we can go to the coffee stand out by the ramada. They added it a while back. They have better java than the cafeteria. Plus, they sell coffee cake from Betty's. Love that stuff. Have you ever had it?" he asked as he hit the elevator call button.

"All the time. There's some back in my mom's room, as a matter of fact. She and Betty are friends. Actually, Betty was here last night when you brought my mom back from the CT. I'll introduce you if she comes back for a visit." Cynthia added, "I could use some coffee. Mom couldn't eat or drink before surgery, and I knew better than to bring anything into the room. She's hangry as it is."

He laughed and gestured for her to step into the elevator first. On the ride down to the lobby, Cynthia asked Eric about himself and how he had gotten started at the hospital.

"I was eating lunch at a burger joint, and the lady at the table next to mine had a heart attack." Outside, he ordered them both coffee and continued his story. "All I knew to do was call 911. By the time they got there, she was gone. I decided right then I wanted to take some courses so I could help someone if it ever happened again."

"I'm not sure I could willingly put myself in the middle of all this trauma and illness."

"You get used to it after a while. The first month I worked here, I couldn't eat when I got home. Seeing all the gory stuff made me lose my appetite."

The barista handed them their order, and Eric led the way to the park bench where Cynthia and Brad had talked the day before. Eric took the seat she'd sat in while she took the one Brad had.

"The next month it didn't seem so bad, and now it's just part of the job," he concluded.

Cynthia wondered what it was like to do a job that had a direct impact on someone's life. Writing a newspaper article was helpful in a lot of ways, but it wasn't always lifesaving. She chastised herself when she remembered how many people the women's shelter articles had helped. Even if she wasn't working in the healthcare field, she was doing something positive.

"Roberto can't stand the sight of blood," Eric confided. "He complains about it a lot. I keep telling him to find another job, but he keeps coming back."

"So, he does talk? I thought he might be a mute."

Eric threw back his head and laughed.

The sound made her smile, and she took the time while he wasn't looking to check him out. He was tall, dark, and handsome, a troublesome trifecta. She didn't want to be shallow, but it was important for her to like a man's appearance. Eric ranked an eight on her ten-point scale. All the activities of his job kept him in shape. His scrubs fit nicely and showed off his well-defined biceps. She'd noticed earlier that his pants, while baggy, pulled tightly over his butt, which appeared to be rock-solid.

Her heart beat a little faster. Maybe this was it.

That's when she heard him call her.

Chapter 31

"Cynthia! I'm glad I found you!"

Despite the fact that an eight out of ten was sitting right in front of her, Cynthia's interest in Eric evaporated when she heard Mark call her name.

Eric looked around. "Someone you know?"

She nodded. "Wasn't expecting to see him here, though."

She didn't hear Eric's response before Mark materialized in front of her.

"Hi." He leaned in, his arms lifted as if he were going to give her a hug, but Eric leaned closer. Mark stopped, then shoved his hands into his pockets and asked, "Any news about your mom?"

She pulled the pager out of her purse and held it up. "This is supposed to let me know when she's out of surgery."

She stood up, and Eric followed. She started to introduce the two men, but Eric's expression changed. Gone was the friendly smile and welcoming demeanor. Instead, Eric's countenance was dark and serious, as if he were protecting his property.

Great. Her eight was a possessive Neanderthal.

She cleared her throat before she added, "Dr. Barr said it

could take two or more hours. It was a complicated break . . . or maybe complex. . . . I forget exactly what he said."

"Good. Not that you forgot, but that she's in surgery now," said Mark. "Barr's a good surgeon."

It dawned on her that Mark wasn't supposed to be in town this weekend. Before she could ask him why he was back, the pager vibrated.

"Wow. That was fast. Mom's out of surgery. I need to get to post-op." She knew she was babbling, but it didn't matter. Cynthia turned to Eric. "Sorry to cut this short."

"No problem. I can walk you back." He dismissed Mark with a curt nod, then gestured back the way they'd come.

Cynthia saw Mark's eyebrows arch. He noticed Eric's behavior too.

"Can I tag along?" Mark asked. "My mom sent me to find out how things are going. If I don't come back with details, there'll be hell to pay."

"Your mother is the sweetest woman in town." Cynthia couldn't imagine Mrs. Andrews getting upset at anything, but she motioned for Mark to join them. "I'm not going to be the one to get you in trouble. It's this way."

Eric stood still while Cynthia and Mark started toward the hospital door. When she realized he wasn't following, she stopped and called back, "Are you coming?"

He shook his head. "My break's over. I'll check in with you later." Without another glance, Eric took off in the opposite direction.

Cynthia didn't know what to make of his behavior, but she guessed he didn't like competition. Part of her felt bad about it, but she was more interested in finding out why Mark was back in town so soon after his last visit.

Cynthia led the way to post-op. "I didn't expect to see you back for a while."

Mark shrugged. "Didn't plan to be back."

"Why are you?"

He stepped to the side as a nurse pushed a patient in a wheelchair down the hallway, and Cynthia paused next to him.

"To tell you the truth, I'm not sure," he said.

Cynthia had spent the week debating whether she should call him or send a thank you note. Mrs. Andrews had assured Cynthia that she'd told Mark thank you and there was no need for anything else, but something felt off. Cynthia had a feeling she'd said something to make Mark uncomfortable.

Before she could decide what to say, he continued.

"How are you feeling since Saturday? Mom said everything went well."

"It did. The article is in good shape." She glanced around to make sure no one was within hearing distance before she turned to him. "Did I do or say something on the way home from the doctor's office last week? I can't remember anything after the surgery, and you were gone before I woke up, and your mother is strangely closed-lipped about the entire thing."

She watched his face closely. When they were in high school, his left eye had twitched if he was hiding something. Sure enough, she saw a slight quiver.

"Out with it. What did I say?"

He took her hand and led her down the hall. "Why don't we find out how your mother's doing? You and I can chat later —not that anything really happened."

She let him lead her down the hall. "But something *did* happen, or we wouldn't be having this conversation." She stopped in front of the family waiting area outside post-op. "Throw me a bone. I'm only going to obsess about it while I listen to my mother complain about her pain. At least give me a hint so I know how embarrassed I should be."

Mark dropped her hand and pushed her hair back from her face. Her cheek tingled where his fingers touched it.

"The nurse thought we were married, that's all. You didn't do a thing. Now, go find out about your mom."

Convinced he wasn't telling her the entire truth, she didn't have time to pursue it as the pager went off in her hand again.

"Fine. I'm going," she relented. "Will you be around for a few days? Can I take you to dinner to say thank you for helping me?" She didn't know how she was going to manage that when she was taking care of her mom, but Mark solved that problem.

"Why don't I bring pizza to you? Carmen's?"

Her stomach growled loudly at the thought of her favorite pizzeria.

Mark smiled. "I'll take that as a yes. Let me know what time and where. My mom said you were going to stay with Cybil for a few days."

She wondered why Mark had checked with his mom, but the pager buzzed again before she could ask.

"Okay. I'll let you know."

Cynthia turned to the post-op waiting room and forced herself not to look back. There were too many things going on right now to start up some sort of relationship with Mark. And she didn't even know if he wanted one. After all, the nurse had caused the confusion. Nothing had happened between them, and she really did have too much on her plate, anyway.

She saw Dr. Barr standing in the waiting room and hurried toward him.

"Everything went well," he said. "She'll be sore for a few days. Observation here in the hospital for a night or two while we watch for complications and start physical and occupational therapy. No more climbing up the attic stairs, though. Someone needs to stay with her to make sure that doesn't happen again. Word around town is you're living over Mary Beth's garage."

She nodded. "I am, but I'll move home for a while until Mom's back on her feet."

"You'll be back over the garage in no time." He winked at

her and gave her shoulder a pat. "The nurse will come get you when you can see your mom."

He walked away, and Cynthia dropped into a chair. It was a relief to know her mother was okay, but what was she going to do about Mark? Something told her she wanted more from a casual pizza date than he did, but she'd figure that out later. Right now, she needed to focus on how she would deal with her mother.

Chapter 32

Per Cynthia's text, Mark arrived at Cybil Anderson's front porch at eight o'clock. He held the pizza he'd picked up from Carmen's Pizzeria in one hand and a bottle of cabernet in the other. He'd debated bringing the wine, but his mother insisted.

It dawned on him that he didn't have a free hand to ring the bell, but the door opened on its own.

"Hi," said Cynthia. Her hair was damp, as if she'd just gotten out of the shower, and she was wearing sweatpants emblazoned with *Glen Valley High School*. "Hope you weren't standing there long. It took longer than I thought to get away from the hospital, and then I wanted to wash the antiseptic smell out of my hair. Come on in."

He walked in, and she closed the door behind him.

"Can I help you with anything?"

He handed her the wine. "Not sure what you like, but this one is a favorite of mine."

Cynthia glanced at it and then led the way to the kitchen. "To tell you the truth, I'm not sure I should be drinking anything. Mom may get released tomorrow, and I need to be on my *A* game. A hangover would not bode well."

He put the food on the counter and turned back to her.

"According to my mother, and I quote, 'Cynthia's going to have her hands full when Cybil comes home. Let her relax a little.' So, enjoy. I won't let you drink too much."

Cynthia laughed. "When did your mother get so wise?" She put the bottle next to the pizza and pulled glasses, plates, and silverware from the cabinets and drawers. "How was the rest of your day?"

He opened the pizza box and put two slices on each plate. "Good. Took Mom to the antique mall. She ended up with some sort of meditation gong. She's never meditated before, but this thing is the key to opening her chakras—at least that's what she says."

He watched as Cynthia opened the wine and poured some for each of them.

"Better her than me," she said. "I tried meditation, but it didn't stick." She placed the food and beverages on the kitchen table. "I hope this is okay. I didn't feel like eating in the dining room."

Once they sat down at the table, Mark asked, "How's your mom doing?" at the same time Cynthia took a bite of pizza.

She moaned. "This is the best in the world. I don't care what my scale says. A treat like this once in a while is good for the soul, even if it isn't good for the gut."

He smiled and waited while she took another bite. As curious as he was about her mother, the look of ecstasy on her face distracted him as he recalled how her lips felt on his. He licked his own lips at the memory.

"Why are your cheeks red?" Cynthia asked. "Did you already have some wine?"

Embarrassed he'd been caught thinking about a kiss she didn't remember, he repeated his earlier question about her mom.

Cynthia scrunched her nose, as if to say he wasn't off the hook, but answered, "She's okay. Probably come home tomorrow. She wanted out today, but OT said not until she passes the mobility tests."

He sipped his wine. "That's good."

"So, why did you get embarrassed a minute ago?"

He should have known better. Cynthia was a reporter, and she followed leads all the time. He decided on the direct approach.

"Two things: One, you kissed me last Saturday; two, I've had a crush on you since high school." He pointed at her sweatpants. "Those bring back some interesting memories."

This time, *her* face flamed up, and Mark almost felt sorry for dropping those two weighty statements at the same time.

She stared at him before taking a long sip of the cabernet.

When she put down the glass, her face was still flushed, but her eyes were sharp and concerned.

"Why don't I remember this supposed kiss?" she asked.

It dawned on him why she would be worried. He raised his hand and shook his head. "You were still loopy after the anesthesia. The nurse helped you into the car and you sort of fell into me. It was a quick kiss. The nurse witnessed it," he added smugly. "You could call her and ask."

"And admit I don't remember doing something I've wanted to do for years?"

Mark did a mental backflip as he understood what she was telling him but stayed calm. They had a few more things to work through before he knew for sure where they stood.

"Which leads up to your second statement," she continued. "Care to elaborate?"

He couldn't tell if she was pleased or upset, so he settled for a playful tone. "Which part? The crush or the sweatpants?"

"Either. Both."

A confession of love wasn't what he'd planned for tonight. His mother would be beside herself if she knew he'd made this evening about him, but Mark felt it was the right thing to do.

"My favorite part of high school was seeing you between classes at our lockers. You always listened, and you were the one person who always told me the truth, no matter what. Not like some of the guys on the team or any of my numerous girlfriends. If I needed something, I could count on you. But I didn't know how valuable that was at the time." He pointed at her legs again. "And those are the sweatpants I gave you when you ripped your jeans junior year. I'm surprised you still have them."

Cynthia blinked several times before she opened and closed her mouth without speaking. Then she picked up her glass again and set it down before she leaned forward and asked, "Why didn't you say something before?"

Mark frowned. She wasn't turned off by his interest, which seemed like a good thing, but she didn't seem to be reciprocating either. He felt like he didn't have a good answer to her question.

"I don't know. You seemed to know where you were going in life, and you didn't need anyone to help you. I, on the other hand, liked having people around. And let's face it—I was a hormonal teenage boy whose communication skills were lacking at best." Then he remembered what she'd said earlier. "Have you really wanted to kiss me for years?"

Cynthia's slow smile revealed her answer, and Mark leaned forward.

"How about we give it another try? This time when you *can* remember?"

Chapter 33

Cynthia licked her lips, then froze when she realized what she'd done. The thought of kissing Mark exhilarated yet terrified her. What if they bumped teeth? What if her breath smelled like pizza? What if this kiss ruined her for anyone else?

"You all right?" Mark asked, his forehead wrinkled. He sat back. "If you don't want to, that's okay. I didn't come over here expecting anything to happen. In fact, I wasn't even going to mention it, but you got that look on your face, and I just . . . blurted it out."

"I do want to kiss you, but I'm not sure now is a great time." She leaned back and took a settling breath. As much as she wanted to know what it felt like, Cynthia didn't think it made sense. "I'm bummed I don't remember Saturday, though."

"It was a good kiss. Great, if you don't mind me saying."

He tilted his head and pursed his lips. She knew he was making a decision about something. He'd done the same thing when they were in high school. Cynthia waited while he came to whatever conclusion he made.

"Why is this not a great time?" he asked.

She inhaled sharply when she realized he wanted to discuss their mutual crushes. Sure, it was possible they might work as a couple, but the downsides to pursuing a romantic relationship with Mark popped into her head: They didn't live in the same city. Her job came first. She wasn't ready to date anyone seriously. She lived in his mother's rental unit. None of those sounded like reasons to start dating, especially if the relationship went south and she had to find someplace else to live.

But the thing that terrified her more than anything was the possibility that it wouldn't work out between them. Then she'd be left with nothing. No connection. No hope. No one. If she didn't pursue Mark, at least she kept her dream of him alive.

"Well, there are multiple reasons . . . ," she began.

He stood up and walked to the kitchen cabinet. His footsteps sounded loud and ominous to her. She cringed when he crossed his arms and leaned back against the refrigerator.

"Okay. And what are those?"

Cynthia closed her eyes for a second to get her bearings. There had to be a way to explain this to Mark that made sense. She hoped what she said was the right thing.

"I didn't know what I was doing when I kissed you," she explained. "You were doing me a favor at the time. Actually, you were doing your mother a favor, and I put you in a bad position. I'm sorry for that."

"Maybe. The anesthesia might have clouded your judgment." Mark's eyebrow went up when he pointed out the flaw in her argument. "But you didn't deny that you've liked me since high school."

"Everyone liked you in high school."

Mark grinned as he uncrossed his arms and placed his hands on the counter. "Now you're just being silly. What's the problem with exploring the possibility of us? We're both adults. Unattached. We've known each other for years and had several disagreements which we've managed to overcome. Why would you not want to see if this could work?"

The words flew out of her mouth before she realized what she was saying. "I'm donating one of my eggs to Brad and Carlton."

Mark froze. The pleasant expression on his face morphed into confusion and something else she couldn't quite read.

"You're doing *what* now?"

She backpedaled a bit. "Brad and Carlton are trying to start a family, and the last surrogate mom backed out. They think it's because they're a same-sex couple. I told Brad he could have one of my eggs for when they find another surrogate. He offered me his sperm if I wanted it—"

Mark held up his hand. "No more details needed there."

She shook her head. "But I don't need it. I'm not interested in starting a family. Just trying to help a friend."

"Let's come back to the family comment later."

She didn't know what else there was to discuss, so she waited for Mark to continue.

"Even if someone else carries the baby, it would still be yours and Brad's biologically," he said.

She shrugged, confused by Mark's reaction. "Well, yeah. That's how it works. Why? Don't you think that's a good idea?"

He raked his hands through his hair, then turned around. She watched him shake his head and heard his fists bounce gently off the countertop.

"Have you shared this plan with anyone else?" his muffled voice asked. "Specifically, your mother?"

Cynthia stiffened. "She knows I'm having my eggs harvested. For some reason, she was concerned about what everyone in town would think of her because of it, but I don't see why it matters. This is my choice, not hers."

"She doesn't know you're donating to Brad and Carlton?"

"No. If I want to help someone, that's my business." She almost added, *"and help my career,"* but she didn't want to make this seem anymore self-serving than it was.

Mark faced her and nodded absently. He looked to be a million miles away.

A hundred different assumptions flew through Cynthia's head, but she couldn't make herself ask Mark why he was upset. She didn't want to know if he was against same-sex parenting or in vitro fertilization or if he didn't want to date someone willing to give away her eggs.

The last reason seemed like the logical answer, but she didn't get the chance to find out before Mark said, "Hey, I've got to go."

Cynthia watched him walk out, confused by the change in his attitude. How could a perfect evening end like this? She needed to know what was behind his sudden decision to leave.

By the time she made it to the front porch, he was outside and halfway down the walk.

"Wait a minute," she called. "You can't just leave without some sort of explanation. I mean, one minute you wanted to kiss me, and now you're out of here. What gives?"

He turned back to look at her. She didn't understand it, but she thought she saw sadness in his eyes as he gazed at her.

"You need to talk to—" Mark bit his lip and looked up at the sky. "Look, I don't know what to tell you. It's just better if I go."

Her shoulders sagged in disappointment. She couldn't believe this was how the night was ending. She wondered if it was her fault, but she hadn't done anything other than be honest about what she planned to do with her eggs. Mark's reaction to the situation didn't make any sense.

"Who should I talk to?" she pressed.

Mark shook his head and headed to his car. "I can't. I made a promise. But you really should reconsider your plan."

Cynthia watched as Mark got into his car and drove away.

She stood there until the neighbors pulled into their driveway and she suddenly felt ridiculous. Rather than explain what she was doing, she marched back inside. She had no desire to explain to anyone that she had been rejected by her high school crush.

Chapter 34

Cynthia didn't have time to obsess about Mark's reaction after Cybil arrived home from the hospital on Sunday. She filed away her former crush as off limits and threw herself into invalid care. It turned out to be a full-time job, even with Helene and Betty stopping by daily. She was exhausted with all the physical work, the emotional strain of her mother's constant complaining, and the lack of sleep, since Cybil needed help to the bathroom several times a night.

She was shocked when she woke up two weeks later and looked at her clock—7:00 a.m. For the first time since Cybil had come home from the hospital, she had slept the entire night, which meant Cynthia got to sleep the entire night as well.

Cynthia stretched her arms over her head and enjoyed the feeling. This morning, she felt almost like herself again. She had always wondered how caretakers and new mothers managed to survive with interrupted sleep. The sleepless nights had left her feeling exhausted and fuzzy, with no concrete idea what was going on around her. She now understood why women took maternity leave. She'd have been a wreck going to work. Good thing Dan had recommended taking some personal leave while she got her mother back on her feet.

Cynthia should send him a cookie cake as a thank you. The thought of him complaining that she was screwing with his diet made her smile.

Stuffing her feet into her slippers, Cynthia took her robe off the foot of the bed and headed to her mother's bedroom. She knocked and then let herself inside, where she found her mother sitting up on the side of the bed.

"Want some help?" she asked.

The physical therapist had encouraged her mother to do as much as she was able but not tire herself out. Cybil must have only heard the first part of the instructions, because never once did she bother to ask for help.

"I can get the walker," Cynthia offered.

"No. I'm tired of that thing. It makes me feel like I'm a hundred years old. There was some surfer who had *his* hip replaced, and he was awake the whole time. And he didn't even use crutches afterward."

Cybil pushed herself out of bed, and if Cynthia hadn't been standing there to catch her, she would have fallen on her face.

"He's a professional athlete who didn't have a complicated fracture to begin with," Cynthia reasoned. "He needed a new hip because of all the extreme sports he did."

"I don't see how surfing is extreme. You stand on a board on the water." Cybil struggled out of her daughter's grasp and leaned on the nightstand for support. "How difficult can it be?"

Rather than explain how much force an ocean wave could exert, Cynthia decided to move on. "I'm going to start the coffee. You want yours in here, or do you want to join me in the kitchen?"

Cybil limped to the closet and pulled her bathrobe off the hook. "Kitchen."

Suddenly, she gasped, and Cynthia rushed forward in case she fell.

"Knock it off. I'm your mother. I can take care of myself."

Shaking her head, Cynthia said, "You're recovering from major surgery. I'm trying to help. But if you want to do this all on your own, fine. I have plenty of things to do right now, one of which is to return to my *own* apartment."

She'd waited to bring up the subject. Cynthia didn't want to start an argument, but she was ready to go back to her own place.

Her mother didn't respond to the comment. Instead, all Cynthia got was demands.

"Leave me alone and go take care of the coffee. Remember, half-and-half. None of that frou-frou creamer you buy. Who needs pumpkin spice anyway? And go brush your teeth. Your breath smells terrible."

Rather than stick around for more insults, Cynthia headed to the kitchen. She flipped on the light and headed for the coffeepot. It didn't take long for the smell of dark roast to fill the air and the first sip to hit her lips. Who needed to brush their teeth when there was coffee?

She poured a second cup, then measured out a tablespoon of half-and-half and put it in a small bowl. Cynthia knew from experience it had to be exactly one tablespoon, no more, no less. How her mother could tell the difference she didn't know, but she wasn't about to risk a tirade.

Satisfied she prepped it correctly, she sat down at the kitchen table to plan her day. Cybil's post-op checkup was at ten o'clock. Once Cynthia got her mother settled back at home, she planned to run to the office to reassure Dan that Helene's wedding dress database would be ready on time. She'd attempted that conversation over the phone, but she felt like a face-to-face was required to convince him. Her second appointment with Dr. Austen was this afternoon. She'd read most of the books and articles on the therapist's reading list but wanted to delve into the subject of surrogacy a little further. Hopefully, she'd have some writing time once she got back.

Her phone rang, and she frowned. No one called her this early unless it was an emergency. Since it couldn't be a family emergency, it had to be work-related. Curious what could have happened to get Dan in the office that early, she grabbed for her phone.

Only the caller ID didn't read the *Gazette*. It was from Dr. Purdue's office, the doctor who was freezing her eggs.

"Hello?"

"Yes, this is Emily at Dr. Purdue's office. I'm calling for Cynthia Anderson."

"Speaking."

"Can you hold, please? The doctor would like to speak to you."

Cynthia stared at the phone as classical music played. If she weren't so worried, she might have complained about the hideous music.

But Cybil walked in and did the complaining for her.

"Where's my coffee? And what in the hell are you listening to?"

Cynthia cradled the phone between her ear and shoulder as she carried her mother's coffee and half-and-half to her. "Doctor's office holding music."

Cybil eyeballed the serving of half-and-half before she poured it into her coffee. That was a good sign. Except Cynthia forgot to bring a spoon over, so she hurried to the drawer to get one in hopes that her mother thought she was planning her actions all along. She set the spoon on the table right as the doctor picked up the phone.

"Hello there, Cynthia. This is Dr. Purdue. How are you doing this morning?" Before she could answer, the doctor continued. "I have some news about the egg donation you want to make. We compared it to the sample that was left for fertilization. Do you know the donor, by chance?"

"Yes. He's a friend of mine. Is something wrong?"

Cybil sat down next to her and asked, "Which friend? What's wrong?"

Shaking her head at her mother, Cynthia motioned for quiet.

"Yes and no." The doctor cleared his throat. "Independently, both the egg and sperm are fine. Either of you will make a good donor for someone else. Just not each other."

Disappointment was the first thing she felt, but then her journalistic nature kicked in. "Why exactly are we not a good match?"

"Match for what?" asked Cybil.

Cynthia held up her hand to signal quiet again.

"The genetic markers are too similar," Dr. Purdue explained. "But neither sample has any abnormalities on its own, so it would be simple enough to find other options. I can put you in touch with the sperm bank I usually recommend, and there are several services for egg adoption for your friend." The doctor cleared his throat. "I'm sure this isn't what you wanted to hear, but it is better to find out about incompatibility sooner than later."

Cynthia took down the names and numbers Dr. Purdue provided, although she frowned when she recognized the names of the agencies for egg adoptions. Brad and Carlton had already tried them.

"Call the office when you make your decision," said Dr. Purdue. "We'll be here when you're ready."

Cynthia didn't bother to explain to the doctor that she would never be ready, that the only reason she was doing this was for her friends. Which reminded her of Carlton. Maybe he was a candidate.

"If I find another donor, would you be able to run the tests again?"

"I can," said Dr. Purdue, "but at this point, working with the sperm bank would give you a better genetic mix. It also takes some of the disappointment out of things. Working with people you know can take an emotional toll that you could avoid by using an anonymous donor. Same thing applies to your friend—he should call the agencies I gave you."

She thanked the doctor and put down her phone. Brad needed to know what had happened, but a quick glance at the clock told her it was too early to give him a call. She'd put that on her to-do list for later.

Right now, Cynthia needed to get over her disappointment and figure out what the doctor meant by "similar genetic markers." She had some research to do since she hadn't thought to ask the doctor for a better explanation.

"What was that all about?" asked Cybil. "Are you sick and didn't tell me? Do you need someone to donate a kidney to you? Because I'm not doing it. I need both of mine. Although I'm sure Eveline will twist that into me being a bad mother. One more reason for this town to hate me."

Struggling to remain calm, Cynthia sipped her coffee. She finished the cup, biding her time before she responded.

"No, I'm not sick, Mom." She topped off her mug from the coffeepot to give herself something to do. "I'm just getting older, which you've pointed out several times, and my eggs are getting older, too. I believe they're called 'geriatric.'"

Triumph replaced the concern on Cybil's face. "So, this egg harvesting story was a failure, then. You were too old?" Then she frowned. "But that doesn't make sense why you needed a donor. What in the world are you up to?"

Cynthia didn't think she could continue this conversation without more coffee, so she turned to pour a third cup.

"My eggs are fine. Nine of them were retrieved. I don't know if I'm ever going to use them, but I ran into Brad at the hospital, and he and Carlton want to start a family. He told me how it's been a problem to find someone to be their surrogate; same-sex couples still don't get equal treatment. Now they found someone who will carry the baby, but she doesn't want to donate the egg. *I have eggs, so I offered to give him one* and, in return, he was letting me document his and Carlton's fertility journey in my story. But Dr. Purdue says we're incompatible, so Brad will have to look for another option."

Cynthia turned around to finish talking to her mother but immediately knew something was wrong. Her mother's face was pale, and she was grasping the chair so hard that her knuckles were white.

Cynthia put down her mug and rushed to her mother's side. "Mom, what's wrong? You look like you're going to faint. Let me help you."

Cynthia pulled out another chair from the table and eased her mother into it. She was close enough to recognize her mother was hyperventilating, something she did when she was overly stressed. Usually something set her off, like the time Cynthia had come home with a shaved head and an industrial piercing in her left ear. But Cynthia didn't know what it could be this time. She mentally ran through the list of things the nurses had said to watch for after surgery.

"Are your legs sore or red?" Cynthia reached down and pulled the robe to the side, but other than the varicose veins that had been there for years, things looked normal. "Remember how Dr. Barr said blood clots can take up to three months to present?"

Cybil swatted her hand. "Stop that," she gasped. "I'm fine. Give me a minute."

"I'm calling an ambulance," Cynthia said.

"No!" Cybil barked, and grabbed her daughter's hand. "I'm fine. Too much standing, that's all. Leave me be."

Cynthia looked down at her mother. Her cheeks had regained some color since she sat down, and her breathing had slowed as well. Maybe it was just the prospect of Brad and Carlton becoming parents before her daughter, coupled with the recovery process, that sent Cybil into a fit.

Cynthia gently removed her hand and went to the sink. "Let me get you some water. Caffeine probably isn't good for you, either." Cynthia filled a glass, then grabbed the thermometer from the cabinet. "I'm checking your temperature. If you have an infection, you'll have a fever."

"I'm fine, I said. I don't have a temperature."

"Then it won't hurt if I check." Cynthia placed the water in front of her and took her temperature. She frowned at the reading. "It's normal."

Cybil pushed herself up and started toward the door. "I told you so. I'm going to my room to get ready for my appointment. We have to leave at nine thirty. Don't be late."

Cynthia watched her mother hobble out of the kitchen and down the hall. She rolled her eyes. Some things she would never understand, including what made her mother tick.

Chapter 35

"Good to see you again."

Cynthia settled herself into Dr. Austen's couch. This time, she had the fortune of not running into Eveline in the waiting area. After the last few conversations with Roger, Cynthia wasn't sure she could keep herself from mentioning to Eveline how high-maintenance he was. Luckily, she didn't have to worry about it.

"I meant to get back sooner, but things got busy," she explained to Dr. Austen.

"Tell me what's been going on. I presume you've had the egg retrieval?"

Cynthia nodded. "About three weeks ago. The information you gave me was helpful as far as what to expect. I found out I'm sensitive to anesthesia."

She blushed as she remembered the complications her behavior had created. As hard as she tried not to, she could still envision Mark leaving her mother's kitchen after their ill-fated pizza dinner. She hadn't talked to him since, and she'd steered clear of his mother. When she needed clothes, she went back to her apartment late at night so she wouldn't run into Mrs. Andrews.

But that wasn't why she was here with Dr. Austen, so she cleared her throat and continued. "Dr. Purdue froze nine eggs. I'd hoped to donate one, but it didn't work out."

Dr. Austen's right eyebrow went up. "Why not?"

Cynthia shrugged. "The doctor said our genetic markers are too similar."

Dr. Austen put her ever-present portfolio on the side table and steepled her index fingers together. "Did the doctor indicate whether you need further testing if you want to start a family?"

The therapist's tone put Cynthia on alert.

"No. He just said I should go through the sperm bank instead of using a private, er, donation."

Dr. Austen seemed to be engrossed in her own thoughts, so Cynthia sat quietly, looking down at the list of questions she'd made during her research. She'd hoped the therapist could clarify a few things, but it looked like the genetics subject had stumped her.

"Could be nothing, but I recommend you find out specifically what the issues are," said Dr. Austen. "If you have some sort of predisposition to a disease, it would be good to know for your sake as well as that of a child's. Now, what else can I help you with?"

They ran through the rest of Cynthia's questions, which focused on the emotional and mental needs people going through the egg harvesting and surrogacy processes needed to address. Having gone through part of it, Cynthia could attest firsthand that many of the therapist's recommendations were on the mark, so she suggested Dr. Austen start an advice column in the *Gazette*.

"This type of therapy doesn't have to be specific to a particular person. All your advice could be followed by just about anyone with some success, don't you think?"

Cynthia thought her reasoning made sense, but she could tell from Dr. Austen's expression that she didn't agree.

"I appreciate that you found my help relevant to you, but I'll pass on the column—or writing a book, for that matter. After we last spoke, I evaluated the reasons why I haven't pursued something in publishing. The more I thought about it, the more I realized how much I value the personal connections with my clients. Sure, I could offer blanket advice, but I don't think that would fulfill me as much as what I do now. Having said that, I am happy to consult with you and Helene."

Cynthia tucked that bit of information away for future reflection. Why the doctor wouldn't want public recognition for her work seemed at odds with Cynthia's own definition of success.

"Well, if you change your mind, you know where to find me." She gathered her things and stood. "I'm heading back to the office now to write all this up. You'll get an email with the draft, and I'd appreciate any feedback on the advice I attributed to you. Otherwise, I think that's it."

"All right." Dr. Austen stood and led the way to the door. "Pardon my curiosity, but how is your mother? I heard she broke her hip."

Cynthia took a second before she responded. Talking about her mother was never fun. Talking to a trained therapist about her mother felt precarious. Anything she said might be examined and evaluated.

"Thanks for asking. Mom's recuperating well. I moved back in with her for a couple weeks, but I think things are going well enough so I can go back to my apartment now."

"Mother-daughter relationships can be full of stress. It's nice to hear you can help your mother when she needs it."

Stress might be an understatement, but Cynthia appreciated Dr. Austen's observation.

"I suppose it's the least I can do, considering it was partially my fault she fell."

"Oh?"

From the tone of Dr. Austen's voice, Cynthia assumed she'd revealed something in her comment.

"Why do you think you had anything to do with it?" Dr. Austen asked.

Preparing herself for some sort of psychological assessment, Cynthia said, "I couldn't help her when she wanted, then she called someone else who couldn't help, either. So she took matters into her own hands, got hurt, and now blames us both."

"Did she say that?"

Cynthia paused. She couldn't remember her mother saying anything of the sort; nor had Brad. As much as Cynthia didn't want to admit it, her mother had been uncharacteristically quiet about who was to blame, which, based on what Dr. Austen said, may have been herself.

"No. She didn't . . . which is the point you're making."

Dr. Austen smiled and opened the door. "I look forward to reading the article. Let me know if there is anything else I can do."

As she made her way to the car, Cynthia mulled over the doctor's comment. She hadn't said anything personal, but Cynthia imagined Dr. Austen did that on purpose.

Maybe, when this article was finished, Cynthia should find her own therapist to figure out exactly what it was she needed from her mother.

Chapter 36

Cynthia let herself back into her mother's house as quietly as possible. After her meeting with Dr. Austen, she had gone back to work for what was supposed to be a few hours but had stretched to 10:00 p.m.

Cynthia hung up her coat and put down her purse before she headed to the kitchen. She'd grabbed a quick salad earlier, but she was still hungry. A quick search of the refrigerator revealed a lasagna someone had brought over, but that didn't sound good. Instead, she filled a glass with cold water to disguise her hunger, drank it quickly, then headed to her room. She might as well get some sleep since she had a lot left to do on her article the next day.

She headed to the bathroom to get ready for bed when she heard murmuring. Cynthia paused. Cybil should be asleep by now. She wondered if her mother had forgotten to take her pain pills or was having trouble getting comfortable. She thought about checking, but she was too tired to engage. All she wanted to do was go to bed.

The house got quiet, so she continued to the bathroom. Locking the door behind her, she grabbed her toothbrush when she remembered something: the bathroom was the best place in the house to eavesdrop on her mother. The ventilation ducts ran between her mother's room and the bathroom, creating a perfect conduction of sound.

Cynthia had done it many times as a teenager. She always knew who was getting detention, whose parents were divorcing, and who was dating whom. Cybil never revealed her sources while she was on the phone, so Cynthia never had to worry about lying. She didn't know where the information came from, but the information gave her power. She knew things no one else did.

On a hunch, Cynthia sat down on the toilet and waited.

"I'm telling you, she's going to figure it out. She's a reporter, for God's sake."

Cynthia wondered what she was supposed to figure out. Were there a few dicey things going on around town she hadn't noticed? Maybe everyone knew that Mark liked her after all. She put her head into her hands at that thought.

"She offered to give Brad and Carlton her eggs."

Cynthia shook her head. What a waste of time—listening to gossip she already knew—when she could be getting ready for bed. Chastising herself, Cynthia reached for the toothbrush again when she heard her mother continue.

"I know. And the doctor told her they weren't a good match. Thank God for HIPAA, but what happens if one of them gets curious? Carlton has a medical background. He might mention something to Cynthia. What if she figures it out?"

Cynthia thought about the day Dr. Purdue had called. Her mother had reacted weirder than normal, which Cynthia had accepted without question. But what if Cybil was worried about something else?

"I don't really care what Eveline thinks, Roger. Why you bothered to tell her is beyond me."

Cynthia's hand trembled as she put her toothbrush on the counter. Her mother *never* spoke to Roger. She complained about him, but never once in Cynthia's entire life had she seen or heard the two of them talking. Based on Roger's recent complaints at the newspaper office, Cynthia understood why he should be avoided, but that didn't explain the current conversation. She leaned closer to the vent to make sure she heard whatever came next.

"She didn't need to know anything about it. You know how she lords it over me. All the time. All around town. If you hadn't told her, she never would have figured it out, and my life would have been exponentially better." Cynthia heard her mother take a deep breath before she continued. "Eveline threatens to tell everyone the truth on a regular basis. How does that make things better?"

Something about the conversation made Cynthia want to go back to the kitchen and make a bunch of noise so her mother would know she was home. The cold feeling that went down her back made her wish she'd never walked into the bathroom, because she sensed that what she was about to find out was going to change the rest of her life.

"What would your boys think if they found out they had a half sister? What do you think Cynthia's going to do if she finds out her father has been living in the same town as her for years but didn't want to have anything to do with her? Huh? How is that going to work in your favor?"

Cynthia's entire body went numb. She couldn't believe what she was hearing. Her father was Roger Gerome. Her half brothers were Brad and Doug. She had part of the same DNA as Doug the Douche, and she'd tried to donate her eggs to her brother.

A wave of nausea rushed over her, but she put her hand over her mouth and swallowed hard. Her mother might hear her, and she didn't have enough information yet to confront her.

She closed her eyes and took several deep breaths to calm herself.

"No, Roger. I don't want anything from you. Never asked you for money or support. Nothing. Nada. Only a promise that you'd keep your mouth shut. And what do you do but tell Eveline? Your wife, of all people. For God's sake! After all these years, she could ruin this."

Cynthia put her head between her knees and hoped the nausea would pass. She couldn't afford to interrupt her mother now. This was the moment of truth.

"Yes, I understand Eveline likes her place in society. That's crystal clear. She routinely reminds me of it."

Memories of her mother and Eveline interacting ran through Cynthia's mind. She'd never understood it, but her mother had always let Eveline have anything she wanted: better seats for the school talent show; hosting privileges for the holiday Bunco game every December; a place on the library board of directors, even though Eveline hated the library and Cybil was a teacher. Cynthia had known her mother didn't get along with Eveline, but she'd never understood why.

Until now.

And as much as she hated herself for thinking it, Cynthia thought Eveline might be right. Cybil had had an affair with Roger and gotten pregnant. With her. And Roger had told his wife the truth.

Roger and Eveline were still together, but the situation had to have caused problems for them. Maybe that was why Doug was so messed up. Maybe Eveline had stopped being a good mother after she found out her husband was a cheat.

"No, this is not her fault. Cynthia was doing something nice."

Her hand fell away from her mouth. Had her mother just complimented her? That was a first.

"Brad called 911 for me after I fell, and they ran into each other. It is a small town, you know."

Cynthia shook her head. Her mother was defending her—also a first.

"Roger, you're an ass. My daughter did not engineer this to get your money. She's more than capable of financing her own life, and she doesn't need anything from you. I've told you that before. She was trying to help, that's all. If I'd known what was going on, I would have prevented it, but I've been laid up with a broken hip, thank you very much. By the way, you and Eveline are the only two people in town who haven't stopped by or sent flowers. So, clearly, Cynthia didn't get her sense of empathy from you."

Leave it to her mother to point out other people's flaws in the middle of a larger argument.

"Listen, Cynthia's going to be home any minute. You need to figure this out, because the last thing I want to do is tell her you're her father. She's got enough on her plate right now. You take care of Eveline; I'll deal with Cynthia."

Panicking, Cynthia let herself out of the bathroom and tiptoed to the kitchen. She took a deep breath, opened the side door, then slammed it as loudly as possible. She grabbed the water glass she'd used when she first came home and refilled it. This time, though, she drank the water as slowly as possible. She wanted to give her mother plenty of time to end the phone call and pretend to be asleep.

Cynthia needed to figure out what she was going to do with this information.

And she didn't think she could keep the shock of discovering the truth off her face.

———————————

Chapter 37

———————————

The next morning, Cynthia hightailed it out of the house and headed back to her own apartment. Cybil put up a stink, but Cynthia reminded her mother that, not too long ago, she'd given her the ultimatum to move out.

"Since when do you listen to what I tell you?" Cybil had asked.

Since Cynthia didn't have an answer to that, she'd grabbed her rapidly packed bag, promised to call later that day, and taken off.

She hoped to avoid Mrs. Andrews when she got to her apartment, but she barely put her bag on the ground when someone knocked on the door. Cynthia didn't want to be rude, but she wasn't up to a conversation. Her excuses died on her lips, though, when she opened the door to Mrs. Andrews holding a mug and a plate covered in aluminum foil.

Before she could say anything, Mrs. Andrews said, "I know you're escaping your mother's house, but I made cinnamon rolls this morning, and when I saw you come in, I brought you some. I'm not intruding, am I?"

Knowing she would stew over the situation if she sat alone, she waved Mrs. Andrews inside. Talking with her landlady relaxed her, and she needed to find some calm about now.

"Cat got your tongue?" Mrs. Andrews asked. "Or is this something more serious?"

"More serious."

"Hmm. I figured something was up if you came back this early on a Saturday. Did you have another fight?"

Cynthia shook her head. "She doesn't know I'm upset."

"I doubt that, but for the sake of argument, what's bothering you?"

Mrs. Andrews made her way to the kitchen, where she pulled the foil off the plate, and Cynthia's taste buds went into overdrive. The cinnamon roll called her, and she took it without hesitation.

"That's what I like to see—a good healthy appetite," said Mrs. Andrews. "Now, I'm going to warm up this coffee, and you're going to tell me what put you in such a fluster."

Cynthia watched while Mrs. Andrews made herself at home in the kitchen. She didn't speak while she microwaved the drink, and then she walked to the living area, where she sat on the couch. From a bag Cynthia hadn't noticed before, Mrs. Andrews pulled out her knitting project. She had come prepared. She planned to get information out of Cynthia regardless of how long it took.

Licking the cream cheese icing from her fingers, Cynthia considered how she should approach the subject. Mrs. Andrews had welcomed her from the start, and she didn't want to change that, but Mrs. Andrews had also been in school with her mother and Roger, so the truth of Cynthia's parentage might not be a surprise to her.

"Why do you think I'm in a fluster?" Cynthia asked as she joined Mrs. Andrews on the couch.

"Mark and I talked earlier this week. I knew something was off when he went home." Mrs. Andrews peered up from the yellow and white yarn she was knitting. "Truth be told,

I'm disappointed in how he reacted, but there isn't a playbook for this sort of stuff. If I'm right, you figured out the truth, and you don't want to talk to your mother about it."

Cynthia put down her plate. "What are you saying?"

"If I were to make a guess, you discovered who your father is."

Cynthia gasped. "How'd you know?" She paused when she remembered the way her conversation with Mark had ended. He'd been upset when she said she was going to donate an egg to Brad. His reaction made complete sense now, knowing what she knew. "How did Mark know?"

The clicking of the knitting needles filled the silence, and Cynthia waited impatiently. If Mark knew about the situation, he had to have found out from someone else, which meant the entire town could be in on the secret.

"Before you get upset at my son, you need to understand he wasn't ever meant to find out. Nor was I. But shortly after my husband died, we came across some old pictures and letters from when Dennis was in high school with Roger and Cybil. Why he kept them I'll never know, but it was enough for us to put two and two together. I asked Mark not to mention it. At the time, I thought it would do more harm than good if you knew.

"There are others in town that know . . . or at least suspect. I'm not privy to the exact count. Eveline, Roger, and Cybil went to great lengths to make sure you, Brad, and Doug never found out. They knew it was a mistake, but after thirty-odd years, it's hard to unravel."

The news that she had been purposefully kept in the dark incited Cynthia's temper. Bursting off the couch, she paced the room.

"How could no one tell me?" she exclaimed. "I've wanted to know who my father was my entire life. I spent my entire childhood being made fun of because I didn't have a dad."

"Would it have been better if you knew who it was?"

Cynthia stopped and threw up her hands. "I don't know! But I wasn't given a choice, was I?" She barely registered Mrs. Andrews shaking her head before she continued her rant. "No, my mother had some sort of illicit affair, and Roger didn't find me good enough to claim."

"That's enough, young lady. No one knows exactly what happened except for Roger and Cybil." She put her knitting back in the bag and patted the couch. "Before you get yourself all riled up, sit down and let me tell you what I know."

Cynthia glared at Mrs. Andrews. "Doesn't it seem odd that *you* have to tell me because my mother isn't willing?"

"Did you ask her?"

"Not recently, but when I was growing up, of course I did. I begged her to tell me about my father for as long as I can remember. When there's no one to take you to the father-daughter dance, you start asking questions. And then, when I saw my birth certificate for the first time, it made me even more determined to find out what happened. No one wants to have an *unnamed* father. But never in my wildest dreams would I guess the truth."

"I'd argue that. Brad strikes me as one person who'd rather not know who his father is."

Cynthia laughed bitterly. "Touché. But that's the problem —I offered an egg to Brad. My biological half brother. What sort of horror movie is that from?"

"I don't know about horror, but I can think of an immensely popular science-fiction series where the brother and sister fall in love." Mrs. Andrews patted the couch again, and Cynthia gave in and sat down. "Nothing bad happened, and the brother and sister remained friends."

"Only this isn't a movie. And the fact is I've been lied to my entire life. My father isn't unknown. He lives in town. He has a whole other family, and his wife hates me."

"That she does, but I wouldn't hold that against her. Eveline hates everyone. Back to the issue, though—Roger

Gerome *is* your father. Why your parents chose not to tell you is beyond me, but they felt it was for the best."

Cynthia leaned her head back on the couch and stared at the ceiling. "So, the reason Mark cut off our date the other night was because he knows Brad and I are related. He should have said something."

"That's my fault," Mrs. Andrews admitted. "But if he had told me why he hightailed it out of town, I'd have turned him around and sent him back to your house. He likes you too much to tell you something like that. That boy of mine got an earful, I promise."

"It isn't his fault." Cynthia closed her eyes. "What a mess. How awkward for him to know what's going on and not be able to tell me." She opened one eye and stared at Mrs. Andrews. "I should be mad at you, you know. You were in on this as well."

"You're welcome to be mad at me. But sometimes people do the best they can with the information at hand. No one was trying to be hurtful. You've had enough of that already." Mrs. Andrews picked her knitting back up and purled. "I should admit something else as long as we're confessing things."

The hairs on Cynthia's neck stood up. She rubbed her neck before she asked, "What's that?"

Mrs. Andrews chuckled as she switched from purl to knit. "*I* renewed your dating contract with Thomas Radcliffe. He didn't want to lie to you, but I didn't think you'd let me do it if you knew."

"Of course I wouldn't have!" Cynthia gasped. "That contract costs five thousand dollars. Why would you do something like that?" She rested her head in her hands and laughed. "Now I know my mother doesn't lie about *everything*."

"Truth be told, I wanted you and Mark to date."

Cynthia opened her mouth to respond but had no idea what to say. It didn't matter, because Mrs. Andrews continued.

"I'm well aware you two liked each other during high

school but didn't act on it. I thought if I could show you what your options were, then you'd be sure to fall for Mark this time around."

Cynthia stood up and paced the room. "You and Thomas picked well. All the dates were duds except for Grady, and he doesn't live in town. How did you manage that?"

Mrs. Andrews shrugged. "That was easy. Thomas doesn't have the greatest selection to choose from. Grady was the best of the bunch, but I figured you wouldn't go for him since he's not from Glen Valley. I gathered you're too busy to travel to meet someone. Thomas agreed that we needed to include at least one decent date, so you didn't quit altogether."

"How did you get Mark to go along with that?"

"Oh, he doesn't know." She looked up at Cynthia and winked. "I came up with this plan after he and Jessie broke up. I'm tired of waiting for grandchildren. I'm no spring chicken, you know."

Cynthia tabled the dating issue. It didn't seem as relevant as learning the truth about her mother and father. Sinking back onto the couch, Cynthia said, "Okay. Tell me what happened between my mother and Roger and how I came to be."

Chapter 38

Cynthia spent the rest of the weekend piecing together the story Mrs. Andrews had shared about her mother. Although it wasn't a firsthand account, what she told Cynthia made sense.

Roger and Cybil had dated through high school until Eveline decided she wanted to be Roger's steady. Even back then, Eveline got whatever she wanted.

"She's always been like that—taking what was someone else's and not bothering to feel bad about it," Mrs. Andrews explained.

"But Roger went along with it," Cynthia countered, "and my mother isn't one to roll over easily. She kicked me out of the house so she could set up a pottery studio, remember?"

"True. But this was thirty-odd years ago, and Cybil wasn't the same person she is now. Eveline and Roger's relationship destroyed her self-confidence. Cybil thought she and Roger would be together forever, and he abandoned her. At least that's what it looked like from the outside."

As much as she didn't want to admit it, Cynthia could see how that would make her mother shy away from any connection with others, including her own daughter.

She waited for Mrs. Andrews to continue.

"Nothing much happened until everyone came back from college. By then, Dennis and I were married and planning a family. He'd kept in touch with Roger, but Eveline's influence was evident by that time. They were quite the item around town . . . ," she paused, "except for a few months one winter, which I think was when Cybil came back into the picture.

"Eveline didn't want to come back to Glen Valley. She hated it—almost as much as Helene Shaw did, but for different reasons. No one particularly cared for Eveline, and I think she got tired of all the bullying and teasing. You could do that back in the day and get away with it.

"Anyway, a few years after we'd all come back to town, Eveline up and left. No one knew where she went. Roger was tightlipped about the entire thing. Cybil, though . . . she was overjoyed and spent so much time with Roger. Tongues wagged. My mama said it wasn't fitting for a young lady to spend that much time with a married man, but it went on for a while.

"Then Eveline showed back up and Cybil left town. When she finally came back a few years later, she brought you. Told everyone that your father had been killed in a car accident, and she came back because she wanted to be someplace where she knew people."

"Then why would she put *unknown* on my birth certificate?"

"You'd have to ask her. Most of us took the explanation at face value, even though there was speculation the timing was perfect for your daddy to be Roger. But Cybil didn't say anything to anyone, and she avoided Roger like the plague. Most folks let it go."

"Oh, come on. This town loves its gossip. How is it possible no one told me this before?" asked Cynthia. "And I'm an award-winning reporter, for heaven's sake. The fact that I couldn't figure it out on my own is disappointing to say the least."

Mrs. Andrews finished the row she was purling and put down her work. "We may be a chatty group here in Glen Valley, but we respect people's privacy, even when those people are difficult. It's up to you to decide what to do with the information, but if I were you, I'd start with your parents."

"What about Brad? I offered to give him and Carlton one of my eggs. Can you imagine what would have happened if the genetic testing had been skipped? It could have ended in disaster. There're higher risks of disease and birth defects. The stillbirth rates are higher. So is infant mortality. And did you know that babies born to siblings have a shorter life expectancy than children conceived by parents who aren't related?"

Mrs. Andrews squeezed her hand. "Yes, I'm aware. Cynthia, there is no guarantee that any baby is going to be healthy. That's something parents take a leap of faith on." She smiled and dropped her hand back into her lap. "You did what you thought was the right thing. Everyone is fine. Yes, Brad and Carlton need to come up with another plan, but as you just said, you're an award-winning reporter. You'll figure out something."

By the time she made it to work Monday morning, Cynthia was no closer to figuring out what to do. If what Mrs. Andrews had said about her parents was true, and Cynthia had no doubt about that, then the people she'd interacted with for years knew her story and had kept it a secret. She hoped they could keep it quiet a little longer until she came up with a plan.

She waved absentmindedly at Jason, who was back to wearing jeans and a T-shirt to the office. The change in attire might have aroused her curiosity on a normal day, but Cynthia had bigger things to worry about.

She dropped her purse next to her desk and started up her computer. The fact that her life was a disaster didn't mean she didn't need to get her job done. The wedding dress database needed to be proofread. It might give her a much-needed distraction.

"Here are your messages," said Jason as he dropped a stack of slips on her desk. Now that he was back in sneakers, she didn't have any warning of his impending arrival. "What happened with you and Roger Gerome?" he asked. "He's called five times today, and it isn't even ten o'clock."

"Who are the rest of them from?"

She assumed her mother must account for the remainder, so she was surprised when Jason said, "Your mom left a few, but most are from Thomas. You've got quite a list of interested men."

She rubbed her temple and shook her head. "To be clear, Thomas is my relationship coordinator—whom I am firing as soon as I have a chance. There are no interested men."

"I beg to differ," said Dan as he walked into her office and held the door wide. "Jason, get back to reception. I suspect we're about to get a visit from Roger Gerome. I'll give you a week off to see RuPaul in Vegas again if you keep him out of this office today."

Jason's eyes brightened at the challenge. "Consider it done."

Dan closed the door behind Jason and then leaned back against it. "Want to tell me why Roger and your mother are so desperate to get hold of you this morning?"

Cynthia's computer screen asked for her password, and she mistyped it twice before giving up and focusing on her editor. "You tell me. Everyone seems to know more than me, anyway."

He nodded condescendingly. "Playing the victim. Interesting choice on your part. My sources tell me you left your mother's house early Saturday morning and camped out with Mrs. Andrews for the rest of the weekend. Roger has been in a panic trying to reach you. I'm surprised he isn't here by now. Word on the street is Eveline is on a tirade. Betty banned her from the coffee shop for a month." Dan folded his arms over his chest. "I'm sure you think this is the end of the world, but you're missing a hell of a story opportunity—could even be better than the egg donation and surrogacy one."

Cynthia narrowed her eyes and stared at her boss. "What are you talking about?" She counted to five so she didn't say anything else. There was no way Dan could have figured out what happened, and she didn't want to say anything she regretted or give him any hints. "My egg story is rock-solid."

"Maybe. But something tells me a story about the girl whose father lived down the street from her but didn't want anyone to know is better." Dan settled himself into a chair and his tone mellowed. "It's been done several times, but this is reality, and you have a front-row seat. Are you really going to let this change things for you? You're on a roll professionally. As far as I can tell, you didn't do anything wrong in this situation. Ignore it or use it, but don't let it pull you down. Then your mother really *will* win."

He stood up as she absorbed his message.

"How . . . how'd you find out?" she asked.

Dan opened the door. "Doesn't matter. What does is that you have a chance to spin this to your benefit. Control the situation before it controls you."

Taking a deep breath, Cynthia considered her options. Dan was right. She could let the story unfold itself, or *she* could tell the story and present it in a way that did the best for everyone involved. That was what a journalist did.

"Can you keep the masses away from my door while I take care of some things?"

He pointed at her as he said, "Only if you promise me you aren't going to let anyone keep you down."

Cynthia grinned. "That I can do."

Chapter 39

Dan's talk spurred Cynthia into action. She spent the rest of the morning calling every place she could think of to find Brad and Carlton a surrogate and an egg donor. If she couldn't donate an egg, she wanted to offer them some options.

The fertility clinic was a bust, but the nurse who answered the phone remembered Cynthia from the retrieval process.

"I know that man wasn't your husband, but why not? There aren't a lot of men in this world who are able to deal with a woman in the middle of a drug-induced hormonal episode."

The embarrassment she felt from her procedure day crept back in, and Cynthia felt her cheeks warm. "It's a long story. Suffice it to say I kissed him on the way home and I don't remember it. I have a lot of regrets as far as he goes."

"If I were you, I'd get over it. But if you don't want to use the resources right in front of you, I can give you the contact information for several placement agencies we use when patients are searching for surrogates and donor eggs."

Cynthia wrote down the information before she asked, "Is this the same information you give to all patients?"

"Yes. Keep in mind that the placement agencies get new additions in the system but don't have time to follow up with everyone on the waiting list. The squeaky wheel gets the grease. Call at least once a week to make sure the staff remember you, but not in a bad way."

The list the nurse gave her detailed several other locations, and one of those specialized in serving the LGBTQ+ community. Cynthia added it to the list of things she planned to share with Brad and Carlton.

She felt even more optimistic after Dr. Austen called.

"Have you changed your mind about writing a column?" Cynthia asked. She didn't have the bandwidth right now to help, with everything going on, but once she got it figured out, a therapy column would be another great addition for the paper and her résumé for recruiting columnists.

"No," answered Dr. Austen, "but I did want to share a new resource that came to my attention: An online registry of surrogate clinics is being promoted through one of the therapy organizations I belong to. I don't have personal experience with it, but I thought it might be of some interest to you for your article."

Cynthia thanked Dr. Austen for the information and, as soon as she got off the phone, investigated the website. Most of the information wasn't new to her, but there were several clinics listed she hadn't heard of yet.

"Every little bit counts," she murmured to herself.

She put together the stack of information for Brad and Carlton and smiled. It might not be an egg, but at least it was a map toward one. Cynthia placed the papers in her bag and headed out the door.

The sidewalk was empty, for which she was glad. She didn't want to be rude to people, but she didn't think she could carry on a conversation as she prepared to reveal the truth about their relationship to Brad. The walk to his office gave her enough time to clear her mind, but she was nervous.

Her hand shook as she pushed open the door. Her nerves weren't helped when she saw both Brad and Carlton in the lobby.

"Hey, didn't expect to see you here this morning," Brad said.

Carlton's eyes lit up. "Does this mean we have news? Are you ready to start baby-making?"

The receptionist coughed, and Carlton rolled his eyes as he turned to Brad.

"I take it you didn't tell anyone about our project," Carlton sighed.

Shaking his head, Brad pursed his lips. "No. You let the cat out of the bag. Sorry, Tammy, I didn't mean to spring that on you, but I'd appreciate it if you didn't share any details right now. We have a long way to go before we're ready to let everyone know what we're up to."

Brad turned back to Cynthia, and her heart broke. He and Carlton looked so happy, and she was about to douse that joy.

He motioned for Cynthia to follow him into his office. "Let's go talk in there."

She walked to the office, with Brad and Carlton following behind her. Rather than sit down, she wandered to the window and looked out. Cynthia needed to prepare herself to ruin two people's mornings.

"It's okay, you know, if you don't want to go through with this," Carlton said gently.

Cynthia whipped around. "Why would you say that? I want to help."

He nodded and took Brad's hand. "We know that. But something about your face says you aren't here with good news. What's going on?"

The tears fell, and before she knew it, Carlton had ushered her to the couch. Brad sat down on one side of her and Carlton on the other.

"It's okay," said Brad. "This is a big deal, and we shouldn't have gotten so excited."

Cynthia put her head on Brad's shoulder and took the tissue Carlton offered. "It's not that. I'd still like to help, but the thing is there's something you need to know." She took a deep breath, dabbed away her tears, and sat up straight. "The doctor called about the genetic testing. He said you and I are not compatible to produce a healthy child."

"What about me?" Carlton asked immediately. "Brad and I kicked ourselves for not having me tested at the same time."

She gave him a small smile as she rubbed her temples. "I asked Dr. Purdue. He can run the same tests on you. It might be a match, which would be great, but I have some other options as well."

She felt someone rubbing her back, and she looked over to see concern in Brad's eyes.

"If you have options, why are you so worried? We'll figure out something."

Carlton handed her another tissue, but Cynthia shook her head. She gave the stack of papers she brought to Carlton instead.

"Here're some details of donors and surrogates. There's an agency listed in here that specializes in surrogacy for LGBTQ+ couples. But that's not the main reason I came over today." Standing up, Cynthia grabbed the chair next to the desk and pulled it between them. "There's something I need to tell you." She took a deep breath as she turned her attention to Brad. "There is a reason you and I aren't compatible. The doctor wouldn't give me all the details, but my mother freaked out when she heard about our plan. I didn't think much about it until I went back to her house Friday night after work. I overheard her on the phone arguing with someone."

The intensity of the men's stares made her nervous, but she forced herself to continue.

"She was talking to your father, Brad. I only heard her side of the conversation, but I put two and two together. The reason my egg and your sperm aren't compatible is because you and I are half siblings. The point is . . . Roger Gerome is my father."

Brad opened his mouth, but nothing came out. He closed his mouth, opened it again, and then flopped against the back of the couch. He remained silent, although he did reach out for both Cynthia and Carlton's hands and squeezed them tight.

No one spoke for a few minutes until Carlton broke the silence. "Roger doesn't even like Cybil."

Cynthia's eyes flew to his, and before she knew what she was doing, she threw her head back and laughed. The sound broke the tension, and Brad and Carlton joined in.

"That's the understatement of the year," Brad managed to get out once the laughter died down. "But as we all know, people don't have to like each other to have sex."

"It helps," soothed Carlton, putting his arm around Brad, "but it is nice to know that you now like half your siblings, isn't it, honey?"

Brad pulled Carlton in for a hug, and for a second, Cynthia felt as alone as she had growing up—the only person in school who didn't have a father. The girl excluded from the father-daughter dances; who had no one to go to work with on Take Your Daughter to Work Day. She swallowed hard. Nothing was going to change the past, but Brad and Carlton seemed okay with the present. Maybe having a brother would work out.

She let out a sigh of relief when Carlton nodded his agreement.

"Really, you're a hell of a lot better than Doug the Douche." He squeezed Brad's knee. "I'm sorry, honey. I know he's your brother, and it really is a horrible thing to call him, but—"

Brad interrupted. "The nickname fits. I get it. While he is

my lame-ass brother"—Brad smiled at Cynthia—"I now have a kickass sister to hang out with. Cynthia, I'll support you however you need. Mom and Dad won't be happy about this, though. Have you considered what you're going to do when people find out the truth?"

Her face flushed. "About that . . . The news may not come as a complete shock to some people. Eveline left for a few months back in the day, and that's when my mom and Roger got together and made me. Mrs. Andrews told me her version of the story. Mark also knows. I haven't asked, but I assume Betty and Helene are in on it as well."

Brad and Carlton looked at each other and nodded.

"Which means the entire town might find out sooner than later," Carlton said. "Gossip is more effective than the *Gazette*, you know."

"I'm aware," Cynthia replied, "but no one has said anything yet, and it's been thirty-five years. So, the question is, do I address this now or let it work its way through town on its own?"

Brad shook his head. "You mean, do *we* address this? We're a team now, whether you like it or not."

"Brad's right," Carlton agreed. "We're here for you, however we can help."

For the first time since she'd discovered the truth, Cynthia understood how it could be easier to handle her problems with a team rather than on her own. Knowing this was the best break she'd ever get, she made her decision.

"Okay, team. Let's face this head-on."

Chapter 40

With Brad in full support of her plan, Cynthia spent the next few days writing her article. It wasn't the one she'd planned, but the surrogacy piece would have to wait. Right now, she needed to tell how one couple's secret had impacted the lives of an entire community.

Discovering half siblings was more common than she thought. In fact, it seemed almost routine as evidenced by some online searches. With the advent of DNA testing, she found pages and pages of stories online about people who had discovered unknown relatives across the country and even around the world.

It was a mishmash of results. Some ended well, others did not. She could see evidence of cheating in several of them, but there were also cases of rape and incest that caused mothers to remove their children from the situations. Some fathers had no idea they had children and would have welcomed them with open arms. Other fathers denied any involvement despite the conclusive paternity test results.

But one thing all adult children who found out they had siblings had in common was that they felt cheated of experiencing a connection with family. Even the adults who had families of their own expressed hurt that they had missed out on relationships with previously unknown brothers or sisters.

Not all the attempts at reconciliation went well, though. One story shared how eight half siblings got into a huge argument, the police came and arrested them, and they all ended up spending the night in jail.

"But we have that shared experience now," said one of the brothers. "Our parents at least gave us that."

When it came time to write her own story, Cynthia drew more from her heart than her head. It wasn't the investigative reporting she preferred, but it was a cathartic coming-to-grips story that pulled on people's heartstrings.

"You better hope it does," said Dan after he read the article. "This is going to blow some people's minds."

"Most of the town already knows about it," said Cynthia, "or at least suspect it. It isn't like people had a high opinion of Roger or my mom anyway. I just want Glen Valley to know it makes a difference to me, knowing the truth and having it out in the open. And for Brad."

Dan shook his head. "I'm going to support you no matter what. You're a great journalist with awards to her name, and you haven't let me down yet. But you're still young, and there are some things that don't change over time. One of those things is that people don't like their dirty laundry aired in public, especially in a small town. It makes them feel vulnerable. It's like a cornered opossum—they're going to hiss and complain, mostly about you to me. *I* can handle it. Can you?"

"Yes, I can handle it," she insisted, although the sick feeling in her stomach said otherwise. "My thick skin came from winning those investigative reporting awards. As I recall, though, opossums don't usually bite. They play dead, which means readers might have some pushback, but it won't be loud—at least not public."

Dan shook his head again. "Thanatosis is a real thing. Have you ever riled up a possum before? They have needle-like teeth and a jaw that can break bones. My brother and I learned that the hard way. Don't mess with a wild animal, even if it looks like it's dead."

"Are you comparing our subscribers to marsupials?" Despite the seriousness of what she was writing, Cynthia found the humor in his analogy. "I can think of several who would take offense to that."

"No one is going to care about that after they read your story." He sat down and looked her directly in the eye. "I'm serious now, Cynthia. Are you sure you want to publish this piece? It is going to infuriate your parents, which will have some backlash on you. Plus, it could change how people see you. You already know what Phil thinks."

The sports reporter had complained to Dan that Cynthia was getting too many perks at the newspaper. "She's never here. Always at the doctor or an appointment, some of which are dates. Did you know that?"

Dan had explained that those were like sporting events.

"Even dates?" Phil had been skeptical.

Dan had nodded. "Even dates."

"She better be careful. If you want to make a ruckus, set up a town scandal sheet. The *Gazette* is a reputable newspaper that shouldn't be used to air dirty laundry. I don't think anyone cares about infertility or dating."

Dan had to point out that all the facts in Cynthia's articles could be substantiated before Phil backed off, but he still wasn't happy.

"She may not have named the parties involved, but anyone with half a brain is going to figure out who they are from your references. If you aren't willing to say it directly, why say it at all?"

"Yes, Phil made his feeling clear," said Cynthia. "And he is shockingly accurate about all his statements, even though he hasn't read this story."

Dan gazed down at the papers she was referring to. "Did anyone tell Doug about this? It affects him too."

She stood up and wandered around her office. "The last number I had for Doug was disconnected. Brad left him a message, but Doug hasn't called back. Brad thinks he's either hiding from someone he owes money to, or he is still mad about being implicated in the Women's Shelter scandal."

Tossing the papers on Cynthia's desk, Dan stood up and walked to the door. "I have to give you credit for being willing to take this kind of heat. It might not win you an award, but it is heartfelt and will stir up emotions—not necessarily in a good way, but it will get people talking." He leaned a shoulder on the door frame. "You plan to talk to your mom and Roger about this? You should tell them about the article before it comes out."

"I left messages. I even shared a draft of the article."

Dan's eyebrows went up. "And?"

Her shoulders slumped in disappointment. She wasn't sure what she had expected, but the fact that neither her father nor her mother had responded made her sad.

"No response. Eveline wouldn't stop complaining, though. She thinks it's a mistake to publish the story. In her words, it won't help anything and can only hurt people." Cynthia grinned at the thought of another conversation she'd had. "Tasha Gerome White supports the article. Since this affects her kids, I wanted to give her a heads-up. She welcomed me wholeheartedly into the dysfunction that is the Gerome name."

"That's right. You have a niece and nephew now."

Cynthia still couldn't believe how much her life had changed, but she was glad for the support that those affected had given her. Brad and Carlton had welcomed her into the family, as had Tasha. Doug was still MIA, but that was probably for the best. All she needed to do now was figure out if she could fix things with Mark.

"When do you want this to run?" Dan asked. "Or do you need time to find a witness protection program?"

The ridiculousness of the question made her laugh. "It's ready to go whenever you need it. I'm heading out of town for a few days, but I really don't have anything to hide."

"I hope that's the case. We'll find out soon."

Chapter 41

"Ladies and gentlemen, we are making our final descent into Chicago. Please make sure your tray tables are stowed and your seatbelt is fastened. We should be landing shortly."

Cynthia checked her seatbelt and asked herself for the hundredth time if making a surprise trip to see Mark was the right thing to do. Mrs. Andrews had made sure Mark would be at his office this afternoon. Betty had packed her a basketful of snacks and sweets to use to convince Mark that he should date her or to assuage her broken spirit if he turned her down.

It was Helene's pep talk that kept her going, though.

"The only reason my daughter, Sara, and I have a wonderful relationship now is because I apologized for my behavior. I flew to Chicago after she moved and told her my true feelings." Helene had put her arm around Cynthia's shoulders. "She could have rejected me, and I was prepared for that. But if I hadn't at least tried, I would have regretted it for the rest of my life. Give Mark a chance. Go to him. I wouldn't have known how to deal with a situation like that, and I'm older and wiser than him."

The plane descended, and Cynthia spotted the runway

below. In less than an hour, she'd be face-to-face with Mark. She closed her eyes and thought about what she planned to say. Earlier that week, she'd emailed the article she'd written to him, but he hadn't responded.

She knew he might be busy at work and hadn't found the time to answer. It also crossed her mind that he had been put in an awkward situation where he discovered something he didn't want to know, that wasn't his story to tell, and he got caught in the middle of things. The Mark she knew would never want to hurt her feelings. Maybe avoidance was his way of dealing with that.

When the landing gear hit the tarmac, she still didn't know what she would say to him. She opened her eyes and tapped her finger on the armrest as she worried about her next steps.

"Nervous about something?" the man beside her asked.

She stilled her hand and moved it to her lap. "Sorry. Didn't mean to bother you."

"No problem. My wife does that when she makes a big decision. Says it helps her think." He shrugged. "Personally, I don't think too much about what I need to do. I just do it. Easier that way. But everyone is different."

The captain's voice on the speaker interrupted. "Sorry, folks, but there is no free gate for us. We'll be sitting on the tarmac for a bit. We'll update you as soon as possible."

A collective groan went through the cabin, but the man beside Cynthia took his phone from his pocket.

"Might as well read something while I wait," he said. "Good luck with your decision."

She decided he had a point, and she grabbed her phone and pulled up the *Guzette's* website. She wondered if rereading her article would give her any clues on how to approach Mark.

The Whole Me

How redefining family changed my life
by Cynthia Anderson, Gazette Reporter

LOOK UP THE DEFINITION OF "FAMILY" *online and you'll find a variety of answers, the most common of which are these:*

1. A family is a group of one or more parents and their children living together as a unit.

2. A family is all the descendants of a common ancestor.

Unofficial definitions of family are found on home decor signs everywhere. Each sign describes family in a different way. A few of my personal favorites are: "A unit that shares goals and values;" "People who love you unconditionally;" "A group you can always count on;" "Someone to drink wine with."

It appears there is a definition of family for everyone.

None of these meanings is a perfect synopsis of what a family truly is, though. It used to be that a man and a woman got married, had kids, and lived happily ever after. That was a family.

Except it isn't. Not for families like mine, a girl raised by a single mom and who never knew her father. Nor for many other families in the in the 21st century who don't conform to the definitions above.

Maybe that's why I delved into other definitions for today's families. This isn't an exhaustive list, but there are adoptive families, childless families, same-sex-parented families, foster families, blended families, co-parented families, and families who used donor sperm and egg to name a few.

The last type of family, those who use donor sperm and egg, caught my interest. Truth be told, a fellow journalist brought the subject to my attention, but once the idea was hatched, I couldn't let it go. I needed to do an investigative piece on fertility and surrogacy and how the nature of family changes with medical advancements.

The story is also why I started my own egg retrieval process. Not only is it important to understand the subjective and emotional impacts of starting a family, but it is also vitally important to understand how medical techniques have changed what it means to have a family. A series of articles will give my firsthand account of what it is like to have my eggs harvested and frozen. I know what it feels like to administer daily hormone injections, to submit to invasive exams multiple times a week, to undergo sedation to remove a part of my body I didn't even know yet. I experienced the agony of "wait and see." Are my eggs viable? Did genetic testing uncover anything? Will I be able to donate to a couple in need?

The stress during this process is something that is unique to each person, but it is a struggle, no matter what anyone says. Even though my journey began as an investigative piece on the ins and outs of the fertility and surrogacy industry, the uncertainty of the process left a shadow over my daily life. Can you imagine what it would do to someone who was desperate for a child?

I'm not interested in starting a family right now. A family is time-consuming, and I'm not at a place in my life that I am prepared to give that effort. It's not fair if you aren't willing and able to give a child what he or she needs. Food, housing, and safety are the obvious things, but time and attention to help them grow and thrive in this crazy world are also essential, at least in my humble opinion.

There is nothing wrong with being childfree. It may not work for everyone, but it works for me. For the time being.

Even though I don't want children, other people do. Lots of other people, as it turns out. Some of those people don't have the options I have. Their desire to welcome children into the world is hampered by some reason. Maybe they are a same-sex couple. Maybe they are single; or a marginalized group; or have medical issues that prevent them from starting a family. There are a whole host of reasons.

I've discovered an underlying strength I didn't know I had. Maybe it is the hormonally-induced mood swings or the fact that my body became a pincushion that is sensitive to the touch. Or maybe it is the realization that the frozen, unfertilized eggs retrieved from my body have the chance to change someone's life. I can give someone an opportunity they could never have.

I believe it is important so that all types of families can be created and thrive. We've come a long way in the medical field, and we have the technology to help people achieve the goals they've set, even the goals that aren't physically possible. My eggs can be used by a same sex couple who want a child of their own. A single man could use my eggs to start a family without having a partner. Those afflicted with medical conditions that preclude them from using their own eggs can benefit as well.

I might only have a finite number of eggs available to share with the world, but that provides a chance for someone to flourish. I'm not the only person needed, though. There is an opportunity for others to help in creating a family for others.

A surrogate is needed to carry a pregnancy to term and deliver a healthy baby. This is a legitimate second job for a person who is ready and willing to share her ability to carry a child to term. Egg and sperm donors are needed. Check out the sidebar to the right for a list of the fertility, sperm, and surrogacy clinics researched as a part of this investigative series. Additional resources will be included with each new part of the series.

I'd be remiss if I didn't mention that, in the process of writing this article, I unearthed the truth of my own family. You might be wondering why I didn't use this angle as the article's lead instead of burying it in the final paragraphs. Reveals like this sell like hotcakes, and I'm sure the news would make for an interesting couple days of gossip around town. Learning the truth about what has been hidden from me for 35 years made it tempting.

In the end, though, everyone makes decisions without fully understanding the consequences. I have the family I need. So instead of muddying the waters, I'm focusing on the one thing I can do: help create another family. I'm running toward that goal, not away from the past.

And so should you.

WHEN CYNTHIA FINISHED READING the article, she skimmed through the online comments. Normally she avoided them, but with nowhere to go and nothing else to do, Cynthia plowed forward.

It was a mixed bag of support and irritation until she got to one from Anonymous:

"When you run toward one thing, you end up running away from something else. Not everyone would be able to handle this situation, but I hope that everything works out for you."

She looked out the window and watched the safety-vest-clad workers milling around outside. They reminded her of worker ants. Everyone had a job and did it without someone telling them how to do it.

What if Mark was Anonymous? Did he really think she was running away from him if she was willing to help her half brother? Why couldn't everyone deal with this situation? Didn't everyone want to be connected?

Cynthia noticed one of the yellow-vested workers motioning toward gate five, and a few seconds later, the intercom sounded.

"I'm happy to report they have a gate for us. It will only be a few more minutes, and we'll get you on your way."

She pushed her phone back into her bag and waited impatiently. Now that they had a gate, and she knew what she wanted to do, she needed off the plane soon. For the first time, she understood why passengers rushed to get off the plane first.

Chapter 42

The taxi ride downtown gave Cynthia plenty of time to decide what she was going to say to Mark. The more she thought about it, the more she was sure Mark was Anonymous, and he believed she was running away from him. She needed to find the right words to make sure he knew that she was ready to stay by his side.

If only she could get to his building, though. Rush hour traffic was bumper to bumper, something she'd never had to worry about in Glen Valley. At its worst, the traffic back home made her hop out of the car and walk.

When the cab finally pulled up in front of Mark's building, Cynthia hurried to pay the driver. As soon as she scooted out of the seat, she heard a man outside calling for the cab.

"Taxi!"

She recognized the voice, and her heart sank. How was it possible she had just gotten here and Mark was leaving?

Making the best of the situation, she held open the taxi door and smiled at the surprise on Mark's face.

"Cynthia?"

Exhaustion from the trip hit her all at once, and the only thing she could think to say was, "Hi. How are you?"

She flinched at the stupidity of the statement, but Mark didn't seem to notice.

"Fine. Great. Confused." He frowned. "Why are you in Chicago?"

As she started to answer, the cab driver called out, "I'm on the clock here. Somebody get in or I'm outta here."

Cynthia pointed at the cab. "Can I ride with you—wherever you're headed? I'd like to talk."

Mark nodded and gestured for her to slide in first. "Airport, please," he requested once they were both seated in the back of the cab.

The taxi screeched into traffic and threw the two of them toward each other. Cynthia's head bumped into Mark's shoulder before she grabbed the handle above the door and steadied herself.

Rubbing his shoulder, Mark asked, "Are you okay?"

She knew he meant from the bump, but she couldn't help but think of how everything had been so crazy since she'd found out about her father.

"Yeah, it'll be okay." She hoped it would be, but she wouldn't know until she told Mark what she had come hundreds of miles to tell him. The cab honked, and she decided she might as well dive in. "The truth is, Mark, I came to see you. Your mom said you would be in town today. I guess she didn't know you were taking a trip."

He looked down at his hands, hiding his face, but she thought she saw something of a grimace. Mark wasn't going to make this conversation easy, apparently.

"Last-minute decision. I've been putting it off, but this morning, it dawned on me that I can't wait any longer. Mom didn't know about it."

Whatever Cynthia thought would happen when she and Mark were together, this conversation wasn't it. For some reason, now that Mark was in her presence, she wasn't sure she could complete her mission.

They drove in silence for a few minutes until Mark cleared his throat. "So, why did you want to see me?"

Cynthia caught the taxi driver's eyes in the rearview mirror. He seemed as curious as Mark.

"Well, I was wondering if you read the article I sent. From the *Gazette*?"

"'The Whole Me'?" he asked. "Yeah. You took a bit of a risk, didn't you?"

"How do you mean?"

The cab driver interrupted. "What's the whole me?"

Mark shook his head. "Excuse me. I don't think this concerns you."

Cynthia put her hand on his arm. "It's okay. He—" She paused and leaned forward. "I'm sorry, what's your name?"

The taxi driver nodded back at her. "Henry, but all my friends call me Hank."

"Thank you. I'm Cynthia, and this is Mark."

"Nice to meetchas both," Hank said as he gave them both a wave.

Cynthia turned back to Mark and paused as she took in the look of confusion on his face. "Hank might as well hear the whole thing. It's pretty public as it stands."

Mark scratched his eyebrow. "I never knew you were so amenable."

She shrugged. "What can I say? I'm turning over a new leaf."

"That was clear from the article."

"What was the whole me?" Hank asked again. "This some kinda nudist experiment?"

Mark's mouth twitched, and Cynthia thought she saw him struggling to keep a grin from his face.

"Let me summarize it for you, Hank," Cynthia said. "'The Whole Me' is the article I wrote for my hometown newspaper. I started out writing a story about the difficulties of egg harvesting and surrogacy. In the middle of researching the article, I found out that the man I planned to donate my eggs to is actually my half brother. And my father, whom I've never met and wasn't named on my birth certificate, has lived in the same town as me for my entire life." She turned to Mark and continued. "The article is what I wrote to let everyone in town know the truth. So now I'm whole. *W-H-O-L-E*. You know. 'The Whole Me.' Does that cover everything?"

He shook his head. "You left out the part about the guy you've had a crush on since high school. How he happened to find out the truth of your father but didn't tell you because he didn't think it would matter since your paths rarely crossed, but when you happened to run into each other again and he's mistaken for her husband, he realizes he still has a thing for you. Only then he finds out you're planning to donate an egg to your brother, but he can't say anything about it without breaking his promise. So, he takes off without a word. *That's* everything."

No one spoke for a few minutes, and the honking of the other cars on the road filled the silence.

"Hmmm," said Hank. "Sounds like an after-school special to me."

The nonchalance of the comment threw Cynthia for a minute, and she asked, "You don't think this is a big deal?"

"Lady—I mean Cynthia—I been listening to other people talk for years. You wouldn't believe the crazy stuff some people come up with. This doesn't even make the top ten." He stopped for a red light and gazed back at them in the mirror. "If this dude's been crushin' on you for years, and you flew here to tell him you love him or something, you might want to get a move on. We're almost to the airport."

Wondering why the best advice she'd recently gotten came from a taxi driver she'd never met before, Cynthia took a deep breath and turned to Mark.

Before she could speak, he asked, "You came here for me?"

She nodded. "Your mom and I had a long talk." She tilted her head. "Did you know she renewed my dating contract?"

"Your what?" he asked.

"I'll take that as a no. Yeah, my mom signed me up with a local dating service. Thomas Radcliffe is the coordinator. The first year it was worthless, but this time around, I had quite a few dates."

"Why would my mom do that?"

"I'll tell you that if you answer one of my questions." He nodded, and she asked, "Is what you said before true? About why you left that night?"

Mark ran this hand through his hair and looked out the window. "I didn't know what to do, Cyn. I promised my mom I wouldn't tell you. My mother isn't someone you break a promise to, but I couldn't stick around and lie either. So, yeah, I left."

"Wimp," Hank muttered under his breath, and Cynthia shot him a look. He shrugged and went back to driving.

"Your mom told me how the two of you found the letters from Roger," she said.

Mark's shoulders sagged. "I'm sorry. Maybe it would have been better to stick around and explain things. Too late now, I guess. Is that why you wanted to see me? For an apology? Because if that's it, I truly am sorry, Cynthia. I didn't mean to hurt you."

Hank snorted.

"Okay. You answered my question," said Cynthia. "Here's the answer to yours: Your mother renewed my dating contract because she wanted the two of us to get together."

Mark frowned. "By getting you to date someone else?"

"I thought the same thing, but you have to admit it sort of worked."

Mark opened his mouth, but nothing came out.

She looked out the window and noticed they were

approaching the airport. "We're almost there. Where are you going to today?"

He stared out the window and didn't respond. She wondered if he had heard her or if he was ignoring her. But as Hank pulled the taxi up to the curb, she heard Mark say, "I was flying to Glen Valley."

Cynthia frowned. "To see your mom?"

"No. To see you. And to kiss you." He twisted to face her. "The last two weeks sucked. I couldn't stop thinking about you. My mom said you would understand, but I wasn't sure you could forgive me. I'm still not sure, even after this cab ride. But you got onto a plane without telling me and found me and told me how you really feel, so I'm hoping that means you'll accept this next thing with an open heart."

Before she knew what was happening, Mark took her shoulders in his hands and pulled her close.

"I love you," he said. "I have since high school. I'd like to make a go of things—together—if you're interested."

Her mouth perked up at the corners, and Cynthia sighed as Mark's smooth lips touched hers, setting off a cascade of electricity through her entire body. His hands moved up to her face and caressed her cheeks.

"Accepted," she whispered.

A car honked behind them, and someone yelled, "Take it someplace else! This lane is for unloading only."

Cynthia and Mark came together for another kiss, surrounded by the honking of the horns, which seemed more romantic than it should have been.

"Guys, I hate to break up the party, here, but I can't stay in this lane forever. Are you staying or leaving?" Hank asked. He pointed. "The parking police are headed this way, so make up your mind."

Cynthia grabbed Mark's hand. "I'll go where you go."

Mark kissed her palm and pulled her out of the taxi. "Let's go home."

Chapter 43

"Are you sure I need to do this?"

Cynthia took the coffee Mark handed her and sipped. They'd made the most of their time together in Glen Valley, but Mark insisted she do one more thing before he returned to Chicago.

"I like things the way they are right now," she said.

He leaned down and kissed the top of her head. "If you don't, you'll always wonder what would have happened."

Cynthia would have rather spent their limited time together figuring out how to move forward with their relationship, but she knew Mark was right. If she didn't try to talk to her mother and father and find out exactly what had happened surrounding her birth, she would always have a tingle of doubt in her mind.

Mark managed to schedule a lunch date for them at Betty's so they could all talk in a neutral location.

"Betty's Sunday brunch isn't exactly private. Plus, most of the town shows up at some point or other," pointed out Cynthia.

"Exactly. The noise will cover your mother's screams and

Eveline's temper tantrum. Or the public setting will be enough to keep them both in line."

The likelihood that either woman's behavior would go unnoticed was slim to none, but she wasn't going to argue with Mark.

Rather than dwell on the upcoming meeting, she put down her coffee mug and reached for him. "How long will it be before you can move back?"

Mark's arms wrapped around her, and he pulled her into a hug. She melted into the warmth of his body and tried not to regret how much time they'd wasted getting to this point. Looking forward was better.

"Not sure. I'm guessing three months tops. I've already transitioned to remote status at work. I just need to get the apartment sublet, but Sara said the Miller Agency has some leads." He nuzzled her ear. "Then I'm all yours. Are you sure you won't get sick of me?"

Cynthia pulled back so she could look into his eyes. They sparkled with his teasing, but she knew the truth. Now that she felt the connection with him, she didn't want to trade it for anything.

She also wasn't excited to leave their apartment when it was time for brunch, but Cynthia knew she could do it with Mark at her side.

THEY PULLED into Betty's parking lot in the convertible Mark had rented, and she couldn't help but suggest, "We could just keep driving. I'm digging the wind in my hair, and you really should get your money's worth out of this car."

Mark turned off the engine and rolled his eyes. "We're going in to brunch, and it is going to be fine. Trust me." He took her hand and kissed it. "Stay here. I'll open the door for you."

She checked out the parking lot while she waited for Mark to walk around the car. Helene and Max Shaw's vehicle sat near the entrance of Betty's Coffee Bar, and Roger and Eveline's town car was parked next to it. She recognized several other cars as well, which made the absence of her mother's car conspicuous.

The passenger door swung open. Mark took her hand and pulled her out. He drew her close before he moved his hands to frame her face. She let him tilt her head so that her eyes met his.

"Whatever happens next, remember I'm here for you. You did the right thing. It's your mother's loss if she doesn't show up. I don't care what anyone says—you are the best, and I love you." He lowered his face, and she closed her eyes as their lips met.

She would have happily stood there all morning, but the door to Betty's opened, and the sound of applause made its way to them.

Mark's lips curved up in a smile. "I think that's our cue." He gave her one final kiss before he turned her toward the entrance and gave her a gentle push. "Let's go."

The coffee bar's regulars seemed pleased with the ruckus that Cynthia and Mark's arrival had caused. Several of them continued their applause, but Cynthia noticed a few of them talking quietly, as if figuring out what was happening.

Betty hurried forward before she could worry too much about that.

"Good morning! I have you set up at the table in the corner. Roger and Eveline are there. Your mom hasn't shown up yet, but Helene and I are here if you need anything." She winked. "I've never seen Eveline this nervous before, and that's saying something."

Before Cynthia and Mark made it across the restaurant, Mrs. Andrews stepped in front of them.

"Mom, what are you doing here?" said Mark. "I thought you were antiquing."

She gave her son a kiss on the cheek, then drew Cynthia into a hug. "Betty and I are leaving after this brunch thing. No one wants to miss the biggest showdown of the century."

Cynthia's stomach twisted, and she turned to Mark. "Are you sure this is a good idea?"

He grimaced and nodded. "Other than the fact that my mother is using this as entertainment—"

Mrs. Andrews interrupted. "I'm not the only one. There's money on the line. Wilbur's put together a pool. Odds are ten to one that Cybil doesn't show up. That's money I can use at the antique mall."

"Mother!"

"What? Everyone needs something to look forward to, don't they?"

Cynthia tapped Mrs. Andrews's arm. "Can I get in on that action? I suspect it's closer to twenty to one."

Mark shook his head as his mother burst into laughter. "You shouldn't encourage her," he told Cynthia. "This type of behavior is liable to be focused on us going forward. You up for that?"

"Honey, this one is a keeper. Remember that, okay?" Mrs. Andrews pulled Cynthia to the counter. "Order and get this party started. We're all going to stay out of your way, but if Eveline or Roger give you a hard time, you've got backup."

The door of Betty's opened. Everyone's heads swirled to see who was coming inside, but there was a collective sigh of disappointment when it turned out to be Brad and Carlton.

"Ouch," Carlton joked as he ambled toward them.

Brad scoped out the room as he followed. "I heard the odds are stacked against Cybil showing up. We had to come see. Although I see my parents are here right on time."

Carlton slapped his partner's arm. "And show our support. And maybe get breakfast at the same time." He hugged

Cynthia and whispered in her ear, "Don't worry about the crowd. You've got this. I'll drag Eveline out by her ear if she gives you any trouble."

She squeezed him back. "I doubt that will be necessary, but I appreciate it." She turned to Mark. "Will you order me a coffee and bear claw? I'm going to talk to Roger and Eveline."

Cynthia left Mark chatting with Brad and Carlton and made her way to the table in the corner where the Geromes waited. She ignored all the people staring at her and focused on her father and stepmother. They both seemed nervous. She noticed the five empty packets of sugar crumbled up next to Roger's coffee mug. Eveline's eyes were glued on the handle of her knockoff purse.

When she reached the table, Roger jumped up, making the cups rattle.

"What do you think you're—" Eveline blurted out, but stopped short when she saw Cynthia standing there. "Oh. I guess it's time for the fun to begin."

Roger frowned at Eveline. "We agreed to civility. Can it."

He pulled out a chair and motioned for Cynthia to take a seat. She hoped the surprise on her face wasn't evident as she slid the chair into the table, but it didn't matter. Eveline's gaze went back to her purse and remained there even when Roger sat down and cleared his throat.

"I'm not sure what you want to talk about this morning or why we had to do it in such a public place."

He glanced around, and she followed his gaze. Most of the other customers quickly looked away, but Mark grinned at her and gave her a thumbs-up. She couldn't help but return the gesture, which caught Roger's attention.

"Really? That only fuels the fire."

"Roger, it doesn't matter what we do right now. This is the most exciting thing that's happened in town since Sara Shaw decked China at the law office. Of course people are going to be interested in what's happening."

Eveline smirked. "Which is why this should be done behind closed doors. No one was meant to know about"—she waved her hand in a circle toward Cynthia—"you. Thank God the circulation of the *Gazette* is minimal. No one really reads that thing, anyway."

Cynthia wished Dan were here to share the recent jump in subscription rates, although that wasn't going to help the conversation. If she wanted the truth, she needed answers. But one person was still missing before they could begin.

Chapter 44

"My mother's running late."

Cynthia glanced at her watch. She'd like to get this over with as soon as possible. They could start now, but she didn't have any desire to repeat any unpleasantries when Cybil arrived.

Roger and Eveline looked at each other. Cynthia registered the smirk that crossed Eveline's face. It was the same one she wore when she was about to drop a bombshell announcement on someone.

Cynthia shifted in her chair and looked pointedly at Roger. "Seems the two of you know something I don't know. Par for the course, I suppose. Care to share?"

Before Roger could speak, Mark approached the table with Cynthia's coffee and bear claw. He gave her a quick pat on the arm before he started to walk away, but Roger called out, "Why don't you stay?"

Mark glanced at Roger in surprise before he turned his gaze to Cynthia.

She gave him a shrug and a quick nod. She wanted someone to sit on this side of the table with her, and it didn't look like it was going to be her mother.

Without speaking, Mark sat in the chair next to Cynthia and took her hand. No one spoke. The bear claw looked good, but the knot in her stomach kept her from reaching for it. Instead, she took a sip of coffee and looked at the door.

"She's not coming," Eveline said, a full smile on her face. "She bailed on you."

As much as Cynthia didn't want to believe Eveline, she wasn't surprised. Her mother had always been concerned about what people thought of her, and having a conversation like this in public felt akin to being an ant under a microscope. Every little thing would be examined and picked apart.

Cynthia glanced at Roger. He didn't seem as sure as his wife. He actually looked uncomfortable.

"Is she telling the truth?" Cynthia asked. While normally Roger and Cybil didn't communicate, things had changed. They might talk daily now, for all she knew. "Is my mom skipping out on this meeting?"

Roger looked at her bear claw and swallowed. "She said she would be here, but you never know. This is something she didn't want to discuss."

"No one wanted to discuss it, and if Cynthia hadn't been so nosy, the secret would still be safe," snapped Eveline. "This is all her fault, you know."

"Hold on, there." Mark shook his head at Eveline.

At the same time, Roger called out, "Eveline, simmer down."

Cynthia looked back and forth between her boyfriend and her father, curious that they both seemed to be on her side.

Mark gestured to Roger to continue.

"Cynthia had a right to know about me," he began. "Cybil and I made a decision—"

"It was more of a mistake." Eveline slapped her hand on the table, causing several people in the restaurant to stare. Eveline glanced around and scowled at the attention she'd drawn. She lowered her voice. "It was a mistake having her come back to this town. She should have stayed away."

Roger's face paled, and Cynthia saw his Adam's apple bob up and down. He seemed distressed, which, in a way, was a good sign. She didn't need a father, but it would be nice if the one she had was on her side.

"As I was saying, Cybil and I had decided she should come back to Glen Valley and raise you here. At the time, we thought I might be able to step in occasionally and be a father figure, but things didn't turn out the way we hoped."

Roger glanced at Eveline when she grunted and slumped back in her chair dramatically.

"Don't you dare blame this on me. You knew all along how I felt, and you went through with it anyway." She crossed her arms over her chest and glared at Cynthia. "It's not like we didn't have our own children to raise. If Roger had paid more attention to Brad and Doug, maybe there would have been fewer problems."

He waved away his wife's comments. "Eveline, knock it off. We're here to talk about Cynthia, not the boys." Roger looked over to where Brad and Carlton were sitting, witnessing the entire conversation. He nodded at them both before he returned his attention to Cynthia. "I am pleased that you wanted to help them . . . even if it did lead us to this." He took a sip of his coffee before he continued. "I won't go into the reasons why this happened. Suffice it to say that Cybil was my first love—"

"And I'm your last," interjected Eveline. "Don't you forget it."

Ignoring his wife, Roger went on. "We did what we thought was best at the time. Neither of us wanted to be together as a couple, so living in the same community seemed like a good idea. It wasn't." He looked at Cynthia. "We should have been honest up front. To be clear, it is your right to tell whomever you want. You could have warned us more about the article, though."

"I disagree," said Eveline. "The entire town did not need to know, that's for sure. I'm ruined!"

Mark finally broke in. "The only reason anyone cares is because you kept it a secret for so long. If nothing else, Cynthia answered a question people have been asking behind your backs. You should be grateful."

Eveline rolled her eyes and pushed back from the table. "I've had enough of this." She pulled Roger's arm. "I told you this was a mistake. It always has been. Let's go before I have to listen to any more of this malarky. Or worse—Cybil shows up."

This time Roger didn't argue with his wife. It was like a switch had been turned off. They stood up and walked out of Betty's.

Mark squeezed Cynthia's hand. "You okay?" he asked.

Before she could answer, Betty strode across the room and said, "Hell, yes, she's okay. She found out what she needed, and it's time to move on." She tilted her head to Brad and Carlton. "I'm not telling you what to do, but those two men still need your help."

As much as Cynthia appreciated Betty's enthusiasm, something felt off. "What about my mother?" she asked. "How is that going to work itself out?"

Betty put her arms around Cynthia and Mark's shoulders. "It may never resolve itself. But you and Mark have a chance that Roger and Cybil didn't take. So, instead of worrying about something you can't fix, why don't you enjoy the relationship right in front of you?"

Betty returned to her post at the counter, chatting with customers along the way.

Cynthia leaned over to Mark and kissed his cheek. "I guess that's our cue. Let's get out of here and figure out what our next break will be."

Chapter 45
THREE MONTHS LATER

"Carlton, stop pacing. It isn't going to make the call come any sooner."

Cynthia smiled at Brad's words. She wanted to say the same thing, but she understood. Today was the day they would find out whether they would be parents in nine months. A baby would change their lives, and she planned to document the entire thing for the *Gazette*.

"I know, but I'm nervous," said Carlton. "The surrogate said she'd call right after her appointment. It was at eleven. It's eleven forty-seven now. Do you think that means it's bad news?"

Cynthia stood up and took Carlton's hand. "It probably means Emily had to wait, and she's going to call as soon as she can."

Brad nodded his agreement.

Cynthia led Carlton back to the couch where the three of them had agreed to tell this child she was its biological mother as soon as it was old enough. There would be no secrets. But she was still as nervous as Brad and Carlton.

"Let's talk about something else for a while," she suggested. "How's work going?"

Brad's eyes opened wide, and he shook his head. "Oh boy. Here we go. Carlton, tell her how busy the chiropractic scene has been since her article came out."

"I'm too nervous," said Carlton as he popped off the couch again and resumed his pacing. "You tell her."

"Helene's been complaining she can't get in for an adjustment," said Cynthia, "but I assumed that was because the wedding venue has kept her busy."

"That," nodded Brad, "and the fact that everyone in town is eager to have their spinal health evaluated by the chiropractor caught up in the middle of the Roger Gerome love-child scandal."

Brad caught the pillow that Carlton threw at him.

"It's not a scandal," snapped Carlton. "Cynthia's standing right here. How can you be so crass?"

"If this isn't a scandal, what is? Everyone in the tri-county area is talking about it."

Cynthia held up her hand for a truce. "It's okay. Several people dropped by my office and said something similar," she said.

She didn't like it, but the fallout wasn't as bad as she'd expected. After her article released, she'd received numerous phone calls and emails saying people had suspected Roger's involvement the entire time but didn't want to say anything for fear of hurting her feelings and making him mad.

"Roger Gerome is an influential man in town. Whoever goes up against him is going to lose."

"I always knew Roger was bad news. It doesn't surprise me that he would alienate his own daughter to keep his reputation intact."

She preferred the positive remarks, though. *"I applaud the way you've handled the situation. Some people would have hidden the facts, but you embraced them, and you've made someone else's life better because of it."*

The anti-Eveline sentiment was entertaining. *"Way to stick it to Eveline. That woman deserves to be put in her place."*

"Dan mentioned we had an above-average number of new subscriptions since the article, so it can't be all bad." Cynthia asked, "What about you, Brad? Any effects from the revelation?"

Brad tucked the pillow behind his back. "Strangely enough, I've had a record number of new client calls. Everyone wants to have their backyard shed designed by me. I'm partial to the clients asking for the barndominiums, though. Those may turn out to be my bestsellers."

Their joint laughter was broken up when Brad's phone rang.

"Answer it," said Carlton as he picked up the pillow and squeezed it tight, then dropped it. "No, wait. I'm going to the other room."

Cynthia snagged Carlton's elbow as he headed for the door. "Stay here. Whatever Emily has to say, it will be fine. We're all here. We've got this." She caught the gleam in Brad's eye and nodded at his phone. "Answer it before it goes to voicemail."

He grabbed the phone and swiped forcefully. "Hello? Emily?"

Carlton's fingers dug into her arm. She'd have a bruise tomorrow, but it didn't matter. All that mattered was that she was here to support her brother and his partner. Her gaze settled on Brad's face and willed whatever happened next to be good news.

"No, no. That's okay. Doctors are always running late." Brad smiled over at Cynthia. "I expected it to be even later than this, to be honest with you."

"Liar," Carlton whispered, and Cynthia couldn't help but giggle. The stress of not knowing was getting to her. She couldn't imagine how Brad or Carlton handled this.

"So, what did you find out?" Brad asked Emily. He listened for a few minutes, his face a blank canvas.

Carlton's grip got even tighter, and Cynthia knew that if

Brad didn't tell them what was happening soon, she'd need a pair of pliers to remove Carlton's fingers.

"All right. Well, thanks for letting us know." Brad paused and nodded. "Sounds good. You too." He pulled the phone away from his ear and looked at them both.

Cynthia was eager to know the results, but from the expression on Brad's face, she didn't think the odds were good that Emily was pregnant.

Carlton couldn't contain himself. "What? What did she say?" He dropped her arm and rushed toward Brad. "Is she pregnant? Tell me." He turned and walked away. "No. Wait. Don't tell me. I'm not sure I can take the disappointment. Whisper it to Cynthia. She doesn't have a poker face and I'll be able to tell."

"Hey," Cynthia objected. "That's not very nice. And it also explains why I keep losing to you."

"That's not entirely why you lose. You're just not a good poker player." Carlton winked at her as if to take away the sting of the insult.

"Are you two finished?" asked Brad. "If not, I have some paperwork to do."

Carlton took Brad's arm and shook it. "Oh, no, you don't. No work until I find out if we are having a baby or not."

"I think you'll want to do this paperwork."

"Trust me, I won't."

Brad's face split into a grin. "All new parents need to do their estate planning. We've only got about nine months to get it done."

Tears spilled down both Carlton's cheeks. "Really? It's really happening?"

Brad put his hands on either side of Carlton's face. "It's really happening," he said, and gave his partner a soft kiss on the mouth before he pulled Carlton into an embrace.

Cynthia watched their embrace and wished Mark was

here with her now. It would be nice to be able to share this experience with him.

Before she could get too sad, though, Brad reached out a hand and waved her close. "We couldn't have done it without you."

Carlton grabbed Cynthia's arm and pulled her into a bear hug. "Is it okay if we ask Cynthia to be the godmother now, Brad?"

He nodded and then added, "You'd be a great guardian, too. If you're up for it. Mark, too, if you think you're both ready for that kind of commitment."

They turned to her and waited for an answer.

Cynthia looked back and forth at the two men, who didn't have to let her be a part of their lives, let alone their child's. She knew Brad's parents weren't supportive of his efforts to start a family and had avoided him since the brunch, but he was still willing to open his life for her and for Mark.

For the first time in her life, she felt like she belonged.

Instead of answering, Cynthia let out a *whoop*. "Of course we'll be godparents and guardians! And I can't wait to throw the baby shower. It will be so much fun!"

———————

Chapter 46

TWO YEARS LATER

———————

"Ladies and gentlemen, that is a wrap for the twenty-fifth annual Journalism Awards Ceremony. Congratulations to our winners, and we will see you next year."

The crowd applauded as it got to its feet, but Cynthia rested her head on Mark's shoulder. "Stay for a while," she said. "Let the crowd thin."

She felt his head lean on top of hers. Losing the award for the investigative reporting category hurt, but she didn't feel so bad with Mark by her side.

"It's Glen Valley," he said. "There isn't much of a crowd."

Brad tapped her shoulder. "The babysitter is expecting Carlton and me back by eleven. I know it's not the celebratory drink we wanted, but we'd like to get one nonetheless."

"She's got the day off tomorrow," said Dan. "If she wants to drink away her misery, she'll have to stay out later than eleven."

Mrs. Andrews scolded Dan. "If she wants to go home early, that's her choice."

"Hear, hear," chimed in Betty. "But my money is on a late night. She already won the boy and the baby. Take the town by storm, I say!"

Cynthia grinned at each of the people around the table. She thought winning tonight would be the most important thing to ever happen to her, but as everyone chattered around her, Cynthia embraced this moment. These people who'd supported her over the last few years showed her what a family really was. The last time she'd won an award, she was alone. She might have lost this time, but she was part of a community now, which felt much better than winning alone.

She smiled as everyone around her argued over what bar had the coldest champagne, where they would have the most fun, and what she should write about next year to have a chance at winning. This was the family she was supposed to have.

Mark squeezed her hand. "What do you think?"

She knew he meant for her to choose a bar, but she couldn't help recalling the argument she'd had with her mother yesterday. They'd only spoken a handful of times since Cybil had failed to show up for brunch at Betty's. To this day, her mother refused to forgive her for article about discovering who her real father was.

"That was a private story that no one should be privy to," Cybil had argued. "You had no right to tell perfect strangers about it. Do you know how it has affected the way parents and teachers look at me? Even some of the students make comments about my ethical decisions."

"It's a good lesson for them," Cynthia countered. "If no one tells the truth about what really happens in life, how are they going to learn?"

"Roger hasn't learned a damn thing," Cybil scoffed. "He lords it over me like it was my mistake and not his."

Cynthia ignored the fact that her mother had called her a mistake and pointed out the benefits of the article. "Would you have gotten as much business at the pottery studio if I hadn't written the article?"

Her mother conceded that point. Cybil had used people's

curiosity about their family secret and turned it into a profitable business. The pottery studio had three locations now: one at the wedding venue, one in Cynthia's childhood bedroom, and one on Glen Valley's Main Street. Not that Cybil gave her daughter credit for that.

Cynthia gave Mark a kiss on the cheek. "This has been the best time of my life. Who knew I'd be dating a wonderful man and be the auntie of a beautiful little girl who I get to spoil rotten and then leave at home with her two daddies?"

Mark nudged her with his head. "Interesting that you've overlooked the other stuff."

Cynthia watched as Mrs. Andrews and Betty laughed over something one of them had said, while Helene and Max had their heads together in a private conversation. She saw Brad take Carlton's hand to his lips and give it a kiss. This was the kind of connection she'd always longed for and what she was sitting in the middle of right now.

It was also the thing she would never get from her father. Accepting that made it easier when things went back to normal.

Roger had resumed his weekly complaints at the *Gazette* about the unfair coverage of his bowling team again.

"I don't cover sports. You need to talk to Phil about it," she reminded him for the fortieth time.

"You should cover them. You're a much better reporter than Phil." It was the closest to a compliment she'd ever heard him utter. He'd stormed out of her office but turned at the last minute. "Remember what I told you: I thought I was doing the right thing. Someday you'll understand that things aren't as simple as they appear. I still don't see how you can hold any of that against me."

The squeeze of her hand brought her back to the evening.

"Hey. You okay? Don't tell me you're regretting staying here instead of moving to Chicago."

The mention of the big city sent a flutter through

Cynthia's heart. Despite offers from several larger markets, she and Mark had decided Glen Valley was home. She would keep reporting for the *Gazette*, but her debut novel was set in a small town, and she had all the raw material she needed right here. Mark's mother had moved into the apartment over her garage and gave Cynthia and Mark the main house. Mark had plenty of room to work from home, with the occasional flight back to Chicago for meetings. Cynthia couldn't be happier.

"Do you regret it?" asked Cynthia. "There won't be award ceremonies every week. This isn't the big city, you know."

"You know what I mean." He leaned down and kissed her softly on the lips. She leaned into it, still in awe of the newness of their relationship. As painful as the knowledge of her parents was, if she hadn't discovered the truth, she wouldn't be with Mark right now. The pain was worth the reward.

Betty cleared her throat and interrupted the moment. "Let the love birds go home and we'll go out for drinks."

Cynthia took hold of Mark's arm and pulled him out of the seat. "No one is going home. We'll all go."

Sliding her arms around Mark's waist, Cynthia closed her eyes and let the warmth and comfort of the situation envelop her. She had found what she was looking for. The people around her might not be what she had expected, but she wouldn't trade them for anything.

Cynthia stepped back from Mark and grabbed his hand. He squeezed it and nodded. This was the break she needed.

"We better get moving." She motioned toward the exit. "We have some celebrating to do."

About the Author

Carole Wolfe writes women's fiction that makes you smile. She enjoys running at a leisurely pace, crocheting baby blankets for others and drinking wine when she can find the time. After moving nine times in twenty years, Carole and her family have settled in Texas.

Follow Carole at www.carolewolfe.com.

Also by Carole Wolfe

My Best Series

My Best Mistake - Tasha's Story

My Best Decision - Sara's Story

My Best Memory - Helene's Story

My Best Gamble - Brianna's Story

My Best Break - Cynthia's Story